A BLOOM

OF

BONES

A BLOOM OF BONES

OF

BONES

A NOVEL

ALLEN MORRIS JONES

NEW YORK, NY

Printed in the United States of America.
10 9 8 7 6 5 4 3 2 1

Ig Publishing, Inc.
Box 2547
New York, NY 10163

ISBN: 978-1-632460-45-5

To my family

Building Fence

Meadowlarks square faint
arpeggios of wheat; dogs piss
on street signs; me I clang metal
to metal, pounding posts the way
sleep pounds us or maybe grief.
A hard unlovely bell pealing the
world to pieces: Mine. Mine. Mine.
Yours.

I SAID, "THAT BIG BULLET went right on through, didn't it?"

It was too cold to snow but still it was snowing; a thin sheet of gauze twisting around the porch light. Buddy kicked through frozen marbles of blood, scattered at them, swept them aside with his boot. He knelt and rose, hoisting the body across one shoulder. Voice muffled by a wool scarf, he said, "Leaking?"

"What?"

"Is he leaking anywhere?"

"I don't see it."

"All right then."

"That big bullet went plumb through, didn't it?"

"Will you quit with the goddamned questions? Just for once?" A gentle man, Buddy rarely cussed, seldom rebuked, never raised his voice. I stood abashed, one breath from tears. He inhaled hard through his nose, shifted the body on his shoulders. "Let's just get this done."

He set off toward the county road, walking fast. I ran to catch up. To the east, it was fifty miles of dirt until you hit the two saloons and five churches of Jordan; to the west, nothing but the Musselshell. At two in the morning, and barring high school kids off on a jacklighting drunk, there'd be no traffic. We had the road to ourselves.

I huffed along beside him. "You ain't taking the truck?"

"You want Pete's blood all over my truck bed?"

"No. I guess that's right."

He glanced down. "You can get on home if you want. No use for us both."

"I want to help."

"All right then."

"Where we taking him?"

"I was thinking Cherry Creek. All them little eroded holes."

"Oh sure."

Our breath bloomed blue around us.

Up on the road he said, "We don't want to leave no tracks. Careful just to step in the ruts."

"All right."

"Just step where I step."

"Okay."

He shifted the body. "It sure turned cold on us didn't it?"

It was so quiet. The squeak of our boots on the snow recalled nails twisting in boards. We were the first or last men on earth. Lone survivors of an epidemic, an ice age.

Eye level in front of me, bouncing against Buddy's back, Pete's shock of hair had frozen into a stiff brush of frost, a rigid, cartoonish explosion of fright. His eyes were open, and a rime of snow had collected in the lashes.

After a time, Buddy left the road. He stood waiting for me to open the gate. Grabbing the post, my gloves came away scaled silver with hoarfrost. He led us a hundred yards or so into the pasture before dropping one shoulder, letting the body slump off into the snow. He stretched his back and studied the sky, the stars showing through. "Looks fair to clear."

It was a porous ground around us now, hidden under the drifted calluses of old snow. A honeycomb of ditches and pipes carved before the spring had been piped and controlled. Buddy began walking in circles, kicking at drifts. "That good round one's around here someplace." After a time, his boot broke through, revealing a vertical chimney as straight as a small highway culvert set on end.

It was deep but narrow. Pete's legs, cocked to the shape of Buddy's elbow, were going to make him half again too wide. Buddy pressed down hard on the knees, trying to force them straight. But the combination of freezing and rigor kept bouncing them back. Finally, Buddy pulled off a glove and reached into his overalls. "Haul one a them legs up here."

I grabbed a heel and raised it, with difficulty, to my waist. Both legs came together, paired in a posture of obeisance. Buddy blew into his fingers, unfolded his knife. He forced the blade under the cuff of Pete's frozen jeans and started cutting. One hard cut up, then another, then he was sawing freely through the wrinkles.

Above all other things, Buddy was a pragmatist. He knew how to keep calm during a crisis. When the grease popped hot across the pan (his own words), he prided himself on approaching the world with the coldest kind of eye.

Now he folded the fabric back to expose Pete's hairy shin and calf. The skin gray, freezing. When he pressed his blade to the soft patch of flesh below the kneecap, that place where a doctor tests the reflexes, the skin split into a narrow, bloodless mouth.

I could see that Buddy had expected this to be a good start, for the skin to pull loose as it did with elk and deer. But human skin, it seems, holds to a tighter standard. He worked his knife hard around the knee, grunting. "Damn if old Pete ain't about as hard to skin as some old beaver. Beavers, now, there's some tough skinning."

Eventually, the blade cracked hard into the joint, popping between cartilage and bone. Buddy worked at it until the leg wobbled loose in my hands. He motioned me away, taking the foot and bracing it on his lap, twisting it hard, heel to toe. Tendons popped and snapped. He twisted it again, then again. Then the leg span freely, caught now only by a remnant of fascia. He cut these last strands away and tossed the leg into the hole: boot, hairy calf, loose athletic sock. Then he treated the other leg just the same.

"Can I close his eyes?"

Buddy touched his dripping nose with the back of his hand. "Help yourself."

Bending down to Pete, I found his pupils fixed and white, frozen opaque. Closing his lids was harder than you'd expect. It wasn't like the movies where all it took was one magic pass of the hand. No. The lids rebounded with a slow, stubborn resiliency. A stitch of thread was needed, or barring that, a pair of coins. I had a quarter and a penny.

The quarter wanted to slide down his cheek. I spat on it and held it in place until the spittle froze. Then I treated the penny just the same. Given the way his mouth was hinged slightly open, the lopsided shine of the coins, his face was given a waggish leer, a wink and grin. He was sharing some private joke. Maybe I was the butt of it. Pete had always hidden his insults inside a jibe. This felt like a proper face for him to take to the grave.

Buddy tilted the body over into the hole, lighter now without its legs, and began stomping at the sides of the hole, shearing off frozen plates of clay with his heels. "We'll come out here in a day or two with a shovel, finish the job. Maybe turn out a few steers to chop up the ground some."

It didn't take long, only a few minutes. Already it seemed impossible that Pete should be down there, legless and dumb.

I watched, surprised, as Buddy next unbuttoned his trousers, dug through his layers of long johns. Finally stood taking a heavy piss into the half-filled hole. Steam rose as if from a crack in the earth. As he turned back, tucking himself in, I expected a grin, a joke. But he only looked old; he looked tired.

Later he handed me the pocketknife he had taken from Pete's trousers. A little deer horn, lock-blade Buck. "Put that in your pocket. You'll need you a remembrance."

As if I would ever be able to forget anything about that night. Or what came before.

THREE THOUSAND FEET OVER Billings, she revisited her uncertainty, touched it like a loose tooth. Why Montana, of all places? Jesus. Montana? It seemed deeply incongruous. Ears popping with altitude loss, she scribbled across her crossword: *Childlessness*. Last year's breast cancer scare. She wrote, "Because I can." She was twenty-eight, and it had been far too long since she had astonished herself.

Three weeks ago, a bad breakup had ripped all the usual holes in her heart. He'd been too self-confident, too wealthy. Publishing never mixes well with Wall Street. Armani suits and Pollini loafers, and while no one could find a better restaurant, he'd had no notion of how to replace a heating element, fix a faucet. She was still attached to certain stereotypes. They should be able to open a jar, for instance. In July, he'd disappeared for a week. No phone, no texts. Turns out, he'd been visiting an old flame in Milan. "There's no big deal here. You're still number one on the hit list."

So that, of course, had been that.

Studying the green-fringed ribbon of the Yellowstone River a thousand feet below, she thought, Mistake? Her father (remembering his death still emptied her heart) had argued that impetuousness kept a person young. In addition to his tight little ears and green eyes, maybe she inherited his flippancy. Not counting phone calls, she'd only met Eli Singer once. He was too old for her. How much did that matter? Just about this much.

They'd met a little over a year ago. She'd been coming from the break room dipping a tea bag, passing Leslie Gordon's office. An up-and-coming agent, gay as a parade, hungry as a cruising shark, he'd called out, "Chloe? Sweetheart? You're from out West, right? Someone you have to meet. Eli? Chloe's in foreign rights. She'll be shopping your book around London here in a few months."

Singer stood to meet her. Only an inch or so taller than Chloe (and she's not especially tall), she noted the long torso, narrow hips. His hair had been inexpertly cut, and still carried the indentation of the cowboy hat he'd left on the arm of his chair. Shaking hands, his palm was thick as a phone book, rough as the flip side of a carpet.

She said, "Sorry, what was your name again?"

A cowboy, twenty-three floors above midtown. He winced slightly as they shook hands, and she noted a split thumbnail. He caught her look. "Missed my dally." As if anyone else in this entire building would know what that meant. But she did. And how had he recognized her?

He had these blue, blue eyes. She admitted an interest. She said, "I can't wait to read your work."

At Leslie's encouragement (what was he doing representing a poet for Chrissakes?), she'd gone first to Singer's most recent book. Fifty-eight poems, gentle and self-effacing but with odd, sporadic eruptions of brutality. He favored a short line, his verses tight as bread pressed into bricks (his own imagery). How could a guy who chewed Skoal come up with this? She began to see what Leslie saw. Leslie, who had a weakness for award winners. This guy could be another Wendell Berry. Or maybe Berry meets Bukowski. In a poem about Sitting Bull's flight from General Miles, Singer described the old Indian finding a fossilized tooth in the eroded face of a clay bank: "A granite canine red and ancient / glittering dark as coals." In fear and frustration, the Indian attacks the bluff, using the tooth to slash and stab at the clay, "biting into fleshless skin." If Eli Singer wasn't famous (as she'd written him in an early e-mail) it was only because he stood outside the circle jerk of gatekeeper academics. "You'd like to think that poetry could stand on its own two legs but it can't." The e-mails led to late night phone calls, both of them drinking. "You know what I love about your work? How you know things. Nobody else knows anything." The suction slip of intestines from a deer, the hot wash of amniotic fluid from a heifer, the weighty obligations of an unfixed fence. "Christ, Singer. If you'd gone to grad school, no way could you be writing this shit."

She was a profane woman. She made no apologies.

For instance: Coming off the plane now, walking down the stairs into the Billings terminal, she opened her arms. "God*damn*. Singer!"

He had a complicated odor about him. She detected truck transmissions, hay fields, horse shit. He stood hip cocked, hat thumbed back, lower lip surreptitiously filled with chew. "Don't know what it is about the Billings airport, how they always takes their time with luggage. Union labor, I suppose."

He studied the airport crowd: the businessmen glancing at watches, young lovers holding hands, fathers crouching low for a hug. "Should be any minute now."

She kept sneaking glances, fighting the urge to stare. Alone in this crowd, Singer was the one you might say was too skinny. A thumb hooked in one pocket, he had the over-large hands and swollen knuckles of a day laborer. It felt odd, hearing the familiar voice coming from this stranger's mouth. Over so many phone conversations, she'd recited the menu of her dating catastrophes, the love/hate thing with her job, talked about her dad. Singer had mumbled assent or denial, rarely offered equivalent asides about himself. She still had only the vaguest outlines of his life. He lived alone, he'd never married. He'd done a tour in Desert Storm ("You know that John Prine song? 'Used to bust my knuckles on a monkey wrench.' I had that goddamn song in my head for two years"). He drove a Dodge; raised Angus-Braunvieh hybrids. "Not so hardy as a Angus but they keep a good weight." He had theories about marbling, fertility. He kept file drawers full of breeding schedules and birth weights. "Biggest problem with most ranches, the way their dad did it is still by god the only way they should do it." But there was so much he'd kept from her.

Her luggage trundled around on the conveyor. A single gray bag with a red ribbon. He grabbed it first. "We're parked a good ways away," he said, "be easier if I carry it." She added outdated chivalry to the list of things she knew about him.

An hour later, driving past Roundup, he turned on the radio. "You mind?" He found an AM station, and sang along softly to Patsy Cline. "South of the buh-order, down Mexico wuh-ay." She turned her face to the window. Yes, this was better. Just his voice.

Past the cracked windshield, the dusty and cluttered dashboard, nothing but flat landscape. "Everything is so *brown*."

"I've been telling folks, we're seven years into a twelve-year drought."

"I see what you mean, about the ancient aboriginal steppe."

He gave her a startled, sidelong glance.

She recited, "The ancient aboriginal steppe, thrumming still with forgotten migrations."

He shifted. "That hadn't happened to me before. Somebody reciting my own stuff back to me."

"How's it make you feel?"

"Let me think about it." He fiddled with the radio. "Yeah, no. I don't care for it."

The bed of his truck was loaded with Costco boxes, industrial-sized bags of flour and sugar, canned beans, a great brick of toilet paper. But as they came into the dusty little town of Jordan—two gas stations, a pair of bars, a squat, glass-fronted IGA—he said, "Need to pick up a few things, you don't mind. Couple gallons of milk."

Inside the store, she found six narrow aisles and two other customers; a matronly ranch wife pushing a cart, a shrunken husband wobbling along beside her. Singer led the way to the dairy case. "Gerald. How you doin? Margie? Afternoon." He put his hand lightly on Chloe's waist. The couple conspicuously failed to return the greeting. The old man scowled. The woman pretended interest in breakfast cereal. Chloe would later have cause to revisit their rejection. For now, she whispered, "Am I a scandal?"

He reached into the milk case for a couple gallons of two-percent. "Got to give them some damn thing to talk about."

"Casanova of Garfield County. How many woman have you taken for a spin through the grocery store there, Mr. Singer?"

"Three or four the last ten years or so. Counting you."

She hadn't expected honesty. "Really?"

"Guess I don't get out much."

She felt the tension. The disconnect, the . . . subtext. Was this a vacation or a seduction? Was she following her nose or her libido? She had recently trimmed her bangs, and couldn't stop trying to hook the newly absent hair over one ear. The movement toward her ear, then the hesitation, had become a tic, a tell. She was aware of how it betrayed her nervousness but couldn't stop herself.

They stood in a brief line at the register. "Hey, Grace. Looking well." He leaned across the conveyer to give the cashier an awkward, one-armed hug. "This is Chloe. Came all the way from New York to see how a Montana ranch works. Chloe, Grace here used to teach me English back in high school."

If it weren't for the hug, Chloe would have thought Grace a man. Short, thin as weeds, white hair going yellow, stray whiskers curling around her ears, the same faded jeans as Singer, the same polyester, pearl-buttoned shirt washed to near translucency. "I never taught you a thing, Eli. Unless it was spelling. You never could spell your way out of a paper bag."

Chloe said, "He's a *magnificent* poet, though, isn't he?"

Grace, bagging their milk, snorted. "I don't know about magnificent. But he could sure write the piss out of a term paper." She handed Singer the bag. "You ask me, poetry should rhyme. Robert Frost, William Blake. Everything else is just . . ." she waved her hands. "Anyway, meetcha, Chloe. Eli, glad you got somebody to talk to down there on that ranch, especially these days." She shook her head. "Good Lord, the things people will say."

It stopped her. *These days?*

Singer was already heading out the door. "Thanks, Grace. We'll see you around." He didn't quite glance back. "Coming?"

She'd had sex for the first time when she was seventeen. That was, what . . . ? Eleven years and thirteen men ago. God, just exhausting to think about. So many first glasses of wine, so many fumbling kisses goodnight. Flirtations and numbers exchanged, first rustlings of cotton and denim, the awkward unzippings, the smell of latex and the inadvertent groans and snorts, farts and sighs. No disease or pregnancy, thank God, just her own increasingly jaded heart.

All the different varieties of men—clothes horses, computer nerds, accountants—and they all dissembled in precisely the same manner. But the act itself? In a secular world, it was her one sacrament. The notion of opening yourself to another human being. A literal opening, of course, but metaphorical as well. The spread of knees and thighs, the unpeeling of skepticism, of irony. It was not to be taken lightly.

He'd tried to clean up for her. In the thick dust of the fireplace mantel, she noted fresh swipes of a rag; the smell of wood polish. She was touched by the effort, amused by the futility of it. His drapes were smudged with dog hair, and a cobweb waved ceiling to lampshade.

She hadn't expected wealth, but the poverty took her by surprise. In the living room, a television but no satellite. An ancient VCR the size of a hassock. No microwave in the kitchen. An overstuffed easy chair and, through a cracked door, an unmade bed and computer monitor, a small desk. And books. Everywhere, books. This, and only this, felt familiar. On the windowsills, tossed askew on the floor, stacked into twisting towers. She found a hardcover of *Station Island*. "Are you a Seamus Heaney fan?" Dog-eared, underlined, it was inscribed to Eli Singer. "With admiration." Fifty miles from the nearest stop light, here was a personal inscription from a Nobel laureate.

They ate in his kitchen. She'd brought several expensive bottles of wine; downplayed their importance even while hoping he might notice. "They're maybe a little bruised, but hey, it's booze, right?" Her and her goddamned insecurities. His table wobbled on metal legs, laminate veneer peeling. She looked down at baked potatoes and asparagus, a buffalo steak swimming in red juice.

He tucked a cloth napkin into his shirt collar. "We got a neighbor raises buffalo. Don't tell anybody, but I've gotten to where I like it over beef."

It was so quiet, she could hear the candle burning. The wind belled at the window screens. "Smells great." She put a small piece in her mouth. Chewed. Glanced up. She couldn't stop being startled by the blue eyes.

He slurped carelessly at the wine.

She said, "That's a '98 Malconsorts." What she didn't mention? Hundred and twenty fucking dollars.

"French?"

"Burgundy. It's not a La Tache, but it's not bad, right?" She swirled her glass. "See how it opens up?"

He wiped his mouth, pretended interest in the label. "Bottle looks fancy enough."

"Uh huh." So that didn't go well.

The scrape of cutlery on dishes, the tick of a grandfather clock. "What's the story with that funny little town you've got there?"

"Funny?"

"I mean, does everybody just wake up in the morning all excited for another day in Jordan, Montana?"

"There's good people in that town."

"Yeah, and I'm not . . . it's just. What do people do?"

"Same as whatever anybody does."

"See, now. No. Now you're offended."

He found his snoose can. "People are just people. That's my opinion. Good ones, bad ones. Scrape out a living here instead of there. Every decision has a price tag. Don't assume people are less than you just because they made decisions you wouldn't have made."

"That's the most you've talked all day. I think I punched a button."

He stood up with his plate. "Ice cream?"

His living room was narrow as a rail car. A floral-patterned couch and tarnished-brass floor lamps and family photos framed in stamped leather. Such an odd little house. They went from wine to whiskey, from the kitchen to his couch, a cushion's worth of space between them. He played LPs on an ancient turntable. Dave Brubeck, Coltrane, Lefty Frizzell. He held the vinyl reverently with fingertips. She said, "New York's got all these vintage record shops showing up. It's kind of a thing. You get me a list, I'll go shopping." Not quite drunk, she felt a tension between them. A guitar string of eventual sex vibrating in a rising note. If they were sleeping with each sooner or later, why not sooner? She stood, touching the arm of the couch to steady herself. "I should get to bed." Her fingertips went to his shoulder, the back of his neck.

His hand briefly covered hers. And if he'd kept it there . . . ? But he took it away. "Good night, Chloe."

She'd brought her own coffee beans (a favorite roaster in Brooklyn), and the next morning she sat with a mug on his back porch, eyes closed against the sun. Fifty yards off, blackbirds flitted through the reeds of a stock pond. A killdeer tiptoed around the fringe. Singer's dogs dozed beside her. He'd said, "Dante's the big one, but Beckett's the one you got to watch out for. Just give him a kick if he gets too close." They were cow dogs, inclined to bite, but she found them charming. She missed dogs. Her fingers found Beckett's head, his ears.

If she lived here, she would take up painting. She would bake, she would read Dostoyevsky. She would plant a garden, shoot a gun. Two thousand miles to the east, New York was waking up to its daily allotments of acquisition and betrayal, reconciliation and violence. The intricate, intestinal movement of eight million people over bridges, through tunnels.

Deep within the house, the phone rang. She jumped slightly. The dogs raised their heads. She clearly heard Singer say hello, pleasantly greet someone named Grady. He paused. And when he spoke again, his voice occupied a lower register, somewhere down next to reluctance. "Well, sure. You think you need to do that, I'm around. You can come on down. I'll . . . eh? He's down in Miles . . . Okay, well. Let me know."

Her coffee turned tepid. The sun touched her shins. Singer emerged in yesterday's jeans and a fresh shirt.

"Just think," she said, "twenty-four hours ago I was calling a car for JFK."

"The thing about jet travel. It takes our souls a few days to catch up."

She liked him least of all like this—when he was aware of himself as a poet, when he played to the crowd. She gestured with her mug back toward the house. "Company?"

"Grady Fisk," he said. Discomfited, he pulled out his snoose can. "Guess you'd call him county sheriff. He's the coroner, too. Just a kid, basically. I knew him back when." He shrugged, maneuvering tobacco around in his lip. "Anyway."

"Sheriff?"

He looked at the pond. "It's bow season. You know that, right? Early September?"

"I think so?"

"Bow season for elk. Well, we had a couple hunters trespassing down on the south side a while back. Turns out, they found a body. This old guy just eroding straight out of the hillside. Damnedest thing."

He was so dismissive, so . . . flippant. It took her a moment.

"I'm sorry . . . A body?"

"Back in seventy-nine, one of our neighbors went missing. Everybody figured he just kind of skipped out on alimony. Pete was such a massive sonofabitch, would have been typical. But now they're saying this is likely him. Dental records and whatnot." He watched her try to do the math. "I was twelve."

"Huh."

"They got a chunk of my ground all roped off with that police tape."

"So do they know who killed him?"

"This guy, Pete. Biggest liar in the world. My old stepdad used to say Pete would rather climb a tree and tell a lie than stand on the ground and tell the truth. Guy was despised pretty much up and down the county. Could have been about anybody."

"So they *don't* know who killed him?"

"I don't guess."

"Is that what the sheriff wants to talk about?"

"What *I'd* want to talk about if I was him."

She flashed back to the grocery store, to the old couple's shunning of Singer. "People think you might have had something to do with it?"

He tongued at his chew, glanced away. "We moved here when I was twelve. You knew that, right?"

"I didn't, no."

"I've lived here most of my life, but I'm still from Billings."

"I don't . . ."

"I'm not from here. That's the crux of it. Pete Fahler—sonofabitch that he was—he was a *homegrown* kind of sonofabitch. They'll want to think I had something to do with it. Even if I didn't."

"So did you?"

He'd drifted away. "Eh? What now?"

"Have something to do with it?"

"Of course not. Hell no."

Sipping a perfectly civilized cup of coffee, she indulged in a moment of romantic decoupling, a little self-conscious reverie. Chloe on the frontier. Her best friend in New York, Helen, recently divorced, had lately taken to browsing through her men like shirts spinning on a rack. "A little advice, Chloe? Keep the numbers on your phone. You need to know whose call you're dodging." They were precise opposites. Chloe knew her pantsuits and had earned her promotions. Helen was a squash player and aesthete of bottled waters. Her money was old. She knew how to cross her legs on a barstool. In high school, Helen had trailed fistfights and flowers; an English teacher had been fired for making advances. She had a carelessness common to beautiful women. She expected to be indulged. "So you think I'm crazy?" Chloe had asked her. "Going off to Montana like this?"

"Absolutely." Helen had Singer's chapbook, and was flipping back and forth between the poems and the author photo. They sat in City Hall Park, by the fountain. "But sweetie, for this man?" She held up the book. "If you don't get on that plane, I will."

"I know, right? But what is it."

"Me, I like complicated men. Remember Ronnie? Good lord god, no, don't remind me. Anyway, whoever wrote this? I wouldn't want to pay his therapy bills, but he's got more going on than fantasy football."

A few days from now they were due to have drinks at a

favorite Scotch bar in the East Village. Concrete floors and a chalkboard drink menu. It would be a chance for Helen to slum it with *Village Voice* freelancers. Chloe had hoped to walk into that bar with the slight swagger that comes from having been pursued and caught. But maybe this was better. A body! Chloe, here in the midst of her own little spaghetti western. Let's hum a lonesome tune. "Quite the vacation you're giving me here, Mr. Singer."

He touched her hand. Those blue eyes. Were they piercing? Why not. "We can get the horses out later, if you want. Go for a ride."

At the beginning of Singer's second book of poems, he had a line: "I want to write about how the knife can turn in your hand." In three volumes, he'd written 192 poems, 2,145 lines. His first chapbook, *An Ax to Earth* (published on cheap newsprint under a truly dogshit cover: wheat stems and a cowboy hat) contained poetry good enough to sporadically astonish. The title poem, a reconsideration of cultural culpability and inherited sin, took the square peg of Günter Grass and pounded him into a western hole.

> *Buffalo Bill and Wild Bill Hickock, Custer,*
> *idolized by toddlers with plastic pistols*
> *disparaged by mothers, but me and you, all*
> *of us, we're still rooted in soil fed under their*
> *festering wounds.*

She supposed, but wasn't entirely sure, that he was

arguing that children can be morally culpable for the sins of their fathers.

In preparing for their ride, she found him out in the round corral, cleaning hooves. His head was bare, and as he bent over, she could see sun damage through the start of a bald spot. He worked with the confidence of familiarity.

She mentioned the poem by name, said, "That one kicked me in the balls, I got to be honest. How do you even start with a poem like that? Did you *know*, for instance, that you were writing a great poem?"

"If it weren't for that book, you wouldn't be here."

"How so?"

"I self-published that one." He straightened, grimacing and touching his lower back, moved over to the next hoof. "Got hold of this little outfit out of Portland. Found them in *Poets and Writers*. Anyway, guy there knew Jim Harrison, and sent him a copy. Jim, he liked a few of the poems, sent the book to Sam Hamill at Copper Canyon. Sam, *he* liked a couple of them. Especially that one you just mentioned. Volunteered to publish the next one, which ended up being *Heartwood*. Which is how Leslie found me, which is how you and me got introduced." He spat. "Big accident, really. Me being a poet."

"Lucky me."

He touched his forehead with the back of his work glove. Half grinned. "Hope so."

The Coyote: Part I

He slipped through burnt timber,
thick fur damp under falling snow, browsing
the day's odors, tender nose tilted to the breeze.
Then hesitated, ears swiveling toward
something amiss.

Me,
a hunter clumsy in heavy boots; musing on
the miracle of the moment. How I was alive here
among the charred branches
under the falling snow.

He scratched an ear, licked at a paw,
tasted the miles traveled since dawn. He had
been here forever, and will be here forever, in the
new snow falling gently
on black bark.

Amen.

THE BEST ADVICE I EVER heard about poetry came from Buddy Singer, who wrote no poems. "Never apologize. Not to nobody, not for *nothing*."

Seeing her come off the plane, I thought: Love is admiration mixed with sex. She had wide shoulders and hips, a healthy frame. She carried herself like a college athlete adjusting to life behind a desk. There was a rhythm to her walking. Her sunglasses weren't quite dark enough to hide her eyes, and when she first hugged me (doing the "mwah" thing, that New York kiss to the cheek), I smelled, in the corner of her neck, a faint odor of sidewalk flower vendors. My first feeling was one of simple gratitude. That she had come to see me, only me. I admired her bravery, just getting on a plane. Not knowing precisely what she was letting herself in for.

Pete's body was found by road hunters from Glendive. A father and son. They pulled off for lunch, sitting on their tailgate, eating sandwiches. The boy had his first pair of binoculars. He couldn't be separated from them. From a distance, focusing, he could just make out a scrap of Pete's T-shirt fluttering in the breeze. "What's that on the edge of the trees down there, do you suppose?" Maybe it was a survey flag. "Go on down and check it out, if you want." The father, fifty pounds overweight and just unwrapping a sandwich, was inclined to be indulgent. Let the kid have his fun. But then the boy was gesturing wildly. Come look, come look.

A few minutes later, at the father's feet, here was a portion of Pete's temple, a clump of well-preserved gray hair. An eye socket, a glint of silver coin. "Good lord."

Pete had been proud of his hair; was always running a comb through it, patting it flat, drawing attention. He'd be pleased to know that it had withstood the years.

The front page of the *Billings Gazette*? "Body Found on Poet's Ranch." The father was quoted, "We both just had this feeling, like something *bad* was about to happen, you know?" The story hit the wires.

The clay, I suppose, the bentonite, had acted as a sealant, preserving the body. That goddamned clay. It scrolls around your tires, collects on your shoes. Everybody in Eastern Montana, we all live in this basin of antediluvian runoff from the mountains. Seventy million years ago we were under water. The mountains are rising even yet, slow as an hour hand. They're mostly granite, which in turn is mostly feldspar, which erodes to clay. And clay erodes, it seems, to tumuli, the detritus of graveyards. Oil-colored imprints of delicate ferns and crumbling, tree-trunk femurs. The surface wants to shed the water but a good healthy cloudburst will peel it back in layers. A geological narrative, plodding doggedly backward. Given enough time, of course, it will reveal everything.

His mother, dead not yet a year and still a presence in the house (bursts of bath soap from the closets, needlework arabesques in the dishtowels) had called him Hiram, but we knew him only by the name stenciled into his belt: *Buddy*.

He had tried to clean up for our arrival, but the residue of filth he'd accumulated since his mother's death was nearly insurmountable. Cookie crumbs in the throw rugs, fossilized jelly stains on the counter, a finger-wide trail of ants marching mudroom to pantry. Buddy himself smelled earthy, like turned soil and fresh milk in a bucket. He wore a flannel shirt and suspenders. Given his narrow hips and sagging belly (parabolas of white cotton T-shirt between the buttons), the suspenders were not an affectation. Nervous, he ran his hands over his graying crew cut. He turned to the kitchen with a flourish, saying to my mother, "You'll be changing things, I guess. Making it your own." Rotten dishes, festering garbage, apple cores.

I was twelve years old. A nail-biter and mouth breather. I had allergies. Buddy took me and Emma into the back of the house, showing us the room where we would be sleeping. My sister affected arrogance, popping gum off my ear. We would be sleeping, it seemed, in a squalid shoebox of dust and dead flies, decorated with framed needlework. An iron bedstead and thin, stained mattress. Under our feet, a raveling runner the color of cheap wine. We were poor, it's true. But I'd never had to share a bed with my sister.

He had made most all of his own furniture, and because he was a poor carpenter, on first impression it seemed that he lived a haphazard, unplanned existence. Square photos displayed in skewed frames. Chairs wobbled in improbable directions. If a pea fell from your fork, it rolled northwest. The home of a transient, we thought at first; a derelict; a man of careless intent. But he was in fact entrenched; he was, in fact, meticulous.

The tour took no more than ten minutes. It was an hour until dinner. What came next? At a loss for further distractions, he showed us his scars.

His only piece of store-bought furniture was an overstuffed recliner. Upholstered in a coarse yellow fabric, glittering with metallic threads, the chair had apparently been fished from a stock pond, or barring that, bought from a yard sale interrupted by a torrential thunderstorm. It still held odors of damp and mold and mud. He sat in it now with the leg of his overalls rolled to one knee. His index finger traced the jagged teeth of a scar around his kneecap. "Barbed wire," he said, dropping his pants leg. He unbuttoned his shirt, showing us his shoulder. "Birdshot." Finally, he jerked off his boot and held up one bare foot, huge and hard as a hoof. "Axe."

Was it meant to be a boast, this exhibition? A swagger? Or perhaps a warning: See, this is what can happen. Or maybe it was an awkward attempt at graciousness. Two small strangers in his house, and in the process of revisiting his own childhood, he'd remembered his own curiosity about someone else's wounds.

I was appalled, fascinated. Emma feigned disinterest, playing with her hair. Buddy wheezed back in his chair, legs planted thick as stumps, big hands spread across his knees. He stared past us at a framed studio portrait of his mother. The old lady glared down, lips pinched tight as a purse. In the corner, his grandfather clock ticked hard. A black-and-white Australian shepherd, Tony, sat by Buddy's chair, panting. Buddy's hand dropped to the dog's head. "Ssss, Tony. Ssss. It's all right. You're okay." Emma pinched my leg, I stared at the floor. We both studied our mother.

My real father tripped off the stage early. I know him only through the warped, one-dimensional lens of early child-hood, flashes like the surprised catch before a movie breaks its film. His name, Seamus, stitched into the synthetic blue pocket of his work shirt; and the vague odors of gasoline, Speedstick deodorant, the sensation of spinning in his hands. Years after his death, his magazines still littered our garage. *Field and Stream, Sports Afield, True.* His appetite was for the pornography of bigger bucks, longer fish. A short man with dark hair and a skin tone all out of keeping with his Irish blood. I have his height and hair but not his skin. Even with his children, me and my older sister, he affected a nervous good humor that led one to believe that he'd once been the butt of jokes, that high school had not been kind to him.

He died by drowning, a death precipitated by rumors of big walleyes on Fort Peck. "Catching them like *this.*" Four employees of High Road Mechanics made the neces-sary phone calls, changed into oil-stained sweaters, lumped themselves together into a 1958 maroon Buick sedan. Two transmission mechanics, a teenage football star from Billings Central, and my father, who rebuilt engines. This has all been described to me. From here, I can only imagine.

There would have been drinking, certainly. Holes chopped through the ice with iron spuds. A bonfire. Hooks baited with bullheads and rods tilted above the holes. A whiskey bottle going around, faster and faster. An escalation of laughter. Reels that jerked and sputtered. Fish pulled out onto the ice to freeze mid-flop. Finally, the grumble of a motor. The ice was certainly thick enough. It should have been thick enough.

There were tracks of previous cars spinning doughnuts. Skids and circles like the fisted doodlings of a child, the orbits of lopsided planets. Laughter, the rumble of the engine. One of the men tossed a whiskey bottle from the window. It began to snow—a twilight gray unfeathering in every direction, erasing the meridian between ice and sky. It must have been beautiful. But they finally ventured out too far, driving over a bubble of warm spring water. The front wheels punched through first, forced by the weight of the engine. The men jerked forward, engine revving, rear tires sizzling. Then they were floating, leaning. It would have happened very fast. Shards of ice splashed against the windshield. The doors were jammed. Within a final, insulated silence, the car sank, tilting gently toward the bottom, coming finally to rest in a settling cloud of silt. They found the car, and three of the bodies, but not my father. He had managed to roll down his window and kick away. I imagine his eyes going black with the spots of his final breath. He's lurching, clawing through the water, finally to smack his fists against a glowing membrane of sky. They never found his body.

No insurance, and he left us with not quite enough money in the bank for a good used car.

My mother was not well equipped to handle the loss. She wasn't fully capable of raising her children, not by herself. We learn these things in retrospect. Of our early years in Billings, I remember most how she and my sister circled each other in a series of fragile, overly-polite truces punctuated by ugly scenes of slamming doors, shouted accusations. Mother had been married less than six months when Emma was born. "You were a mistake, Emma. I've told you that, haven't I?"

There weren't many jobs for women in Montana in the seventies. Nurse or school teacher, hair stylist or housekeeper. Our mother cut hair. Standing at her station Tuesdays through Saturdays, ten to six, she winced over her lower back, shifted on fallen arches. Growing up in Butte, she'd wanted most of all to be an artist. "Georgia O'Keefe, only without the porn." She'd had a talent for sketching, and still kept scrapbooks. Sunset over the pit. A mule deer. Studies of a housecat.

In retribution, or perhaps out of jealousy (as Emma aged and began attracting glances), my mother put her foot down. "I ever catch you alone in a house with a grown man, girly? You'll be out on the street before you can say two-bit whore." My mother was in her early thirties, an age when some women struggle against their fading youth. At a time when miniskirts were all the rage, when hot-curled, Farrah-Fawcett hair was de rigueur, Mother dressed Emma in floral-print prairie skirts and forced her into the braids of a sixties folk singer. "You're still young enough, I'll send you to the children's farm. Don't think I won't." The children's farm was a theme throughout our childhoods, her persistent threat.

Emma said, "I don't think there is such a place."

"A lot you know, missy."

Once or twice a month (Mother's snores rising from the next room), Emma would open her window and unclip the screen, straddle the sill, reach across to the lattice of dead ivy and slip away. An hour later, smelling of cigarettes, she would return to wake me up, sit Indian-wise on my floor, sorting through shoplifted tubes of lipstick, tiny jars of eyeliner. She'd hand me candy bars—"This is for you"—which I would eat in impressed silence. I was the last person in the world who wanted to see her in trouble. I was the conciliator, the peacemaker. I told lies on behalf of an imagined peace.

Mother had her moments of generosity. We would sometimes climb into our station wagon and drive up to the rims to watch the planes land. This was, at least in part, a reflection of our financial condition, of a time when even the fifty cents for a matinee sent us digging through the couch cushions. But in some ways the airport was better than a movie. We stared through finger-smudged windows as cathedrals of silver left the earth in defiance of gravity and reason. Mother ignored the planes, opting instead for the discarded magazines and newspapers, reading the horoscopes with an avidity that drew attention to itself. Scoffing, laughing in delight. She sat with her shoes kicked off and her legs curled up, glancing at the arriving passengers. The elaborate grins and waiting hugs. The dropped luggage and rush to Grandma. And while the delight my sister and I found in airports was of the sort that could be had under any big top (elaborate miracles for small fees), the attractions my mother felt were almost certainly familial, the envy of homecomings. Not yet as old as we thought her, not unattractive, when the cycles of her depression gave way to frivolity, she would spend at least one evening a week out dancing. She would model for us her nicest dresses, ask our opinions. She had a small record player in a pink case, and on these good evenings she would play Allman Brothers 45s and dance from one dress to another. During a brief period—after babysitters, but before the loss of incredulity—Emma and I would sit and applaud or make expressions of distaste that were meant only to exaggerate her laughter. More than a few of these nights, of course, ended with Mother fumbling at the front door, giggling; a strange man snatching at her from behind.

Given her fondness for horoscopes, newspapers, it's maybe appropriate that she found our new lives in a classified ad. Lost in a wad of packaging, twisted around a thrift store lamp, half an inch of understated hope and subsumed loneliness. She cut it out and kept it by the phone for a week before calling for an interview: "Housekeeper wanted, Rattletrap Ranch, Jordan. Rm & Brd included. Good pay. Kids (especially Boys) okay." In later years, I would try to imagine Buddy at his off-kilter kitchen table, scribbling different versions of this ad. All the time he would have been feeling his mother's disapproval. What an effort, what a great effort it must have been.

I'm sure it was difficult for Mother, too. Her last day in the hair salon. A scattering of clippings on tile, the soothing odors of sprays and gels, the balloons they'd brought to her station. It had not been a happy place for her but it did have the comfort of habit.

When she drove us north, everything we owned fit into the back of the wagon. Three hours on pavement, another on gravel. Like sailing or swimming, our progress was so slow as to seem nonexistent. The horizon remained at a constant remove. Gradually, however, the farm ground crumbled away, folding into a pine-furzed jumble of eroded hills, knobs and coulees.

In late afternoon, we came to a split in the road. There was a view. She stopped the car, sitting for a moment gripping the wheel. Our contrail of dust caught up to us, sending pale clouds past the windows. To the north, a double-wide trailer house, a rusty swingset. She said, "That's where you'll be going to school."

What had seemed quaint suddenly turned squalid.

Was my mother uncertain? She turned off the engine and stepped outside to smoke a cigarette. Was she questioning herself? Reassessing those stars and star alignments that had brought us to this pass? While she smoked, Emma and I kicked through the weeds beside the road. Emma said, "There's arrowheads all through this country." Eventually, my mother flicked her cigarette away and, with small motions of her fingers, brought us into a hug, clutching us hard, kissing our cheeks, one and then the other. "My soldiers, my dear brave little soldiers."

Despite everything, this was, I think, a good day for her.

Everybody's got too much time on their hands. That's what it comes down to. Twelve hundred people in this county. Three preachers, ten bartenders, a couple dozen top-notch diesel mechanics. A courthouse stuffed full of file clerks and rubber stampers. And all of us busiest when we're minding each other's affairs.

History here is only a century thick. Telling a story, you can start at the beginning. A lifetime of wind and drought, childbirth and suicide. Here's where it warps you, here's where it strengthens you. When those hunters found Pete Fahler's body, it made things awful quiet for a while. Quiet, then considerably louder. Allegiances shifted, blame was reconsidered. Pete was not the sonofabitch they had believed him to be.

Pete's son, Curt—even at thirty-five, even with three children of his own—was still a spoiled toddler, a little boy who threw playground tantrums. Granted, it must have been hard growing up without a father. No calls, no letters. Just sporadic wads of cash appearing through the mail. Curt learned by example: Money is the opposite of guilt. The payments came in envelopes postmarked Billings, the address handwritten in block letters. For a man who despised his father, every envelope was a punch in the nose. Two hundred bucks here, five hundred bucks there, it added up. The twins needed braces. His ranch truck dropped a transmission. The old man would be seventy, seventy-five years old now. Wasn't he curious about his grandkids? If times weren't so hard, Curt would have just tossed the cash in the furnace. But times were hard. It was a bitter pill, swallowed on a near-daily basis.

When Pete's body eroded out of the hillside, Grady Fisk called Curt. "You need to meet me down on Cherry Creek." And while this was not an especially unusual occurrence (the Breaks keep releasing ancient bodies; skulls and teeth and finger bones, copper kettles and stone axes and medicine bundles) the list of people with names gone missing in Garfield County was only a few lines long.

Grady and his deputy worked with shovel and pick while Curt hunkered on his heels, smoking. Grady tossed him a leather wallet. "Look familiar?" A gritty fold of leather filled with twenty-three dollars of antique cash. "Yeah, that's his." Grady and his deputy gingerly lifted the curled corpse into a body bag, the desiccated bones held stiffly together by the leathered skin, lips stretched back to reveal yellow, horsey teeth. The eyes were sunk knuckle deep into the skull and his hands were drawn in like claws. Then the legs. Each one needed a separate trip back into the hole. "Goddamn, Grady. Who'd do such a thing?" Curt was close to tears.

"We'll get him." But it was only talk. Grady had been in this job for two years. Before that, he'd been a roughneck down in Kemmerer. Fisks are one of the three families in the county with enough votes to sway any election, elect whichever cousin cares to attach himself to the government teat. Grady ran unopposed, but to his credit worked the job in good faith. A decent man. He'd gone to Helena to learn how to handle a crime scene, collect evidence. Rubber gloves and Ziploc baggies, Luminol and Locard's exchange principle. Whole nine yards. But they'd never talked about murder scenes that were thirty years gone.

He stretched the body bag out on his tailgate. The whole package smaller than you'd think. This is what we all boil down to. A wad of dried husks. Grady zipped the bag up to the corpse's sternum, then paused. A patch of the grave-rotted T-shirt seemed stained a slightly darker brown. He used a pencil to pull back a scrap, reveal a collarbone, a xylophone-scroll of ribcage.

Peering over his shoulder, Curt said, "Is that a bullet hole?"

Mistake, inviting Curt to the crime scene. He could see it now. Rookie mistake. Grady was always berating himself for these types of errors. Was the job too big for him? He looked at Curt and saw how easily grief could segue to anger, anger to violence. "We'll do an autopsy. I'll let you know."

"It is, isn't it? A goddamned bullet hole." He touched his eyes with the back of a wrist.

"Curt."

"I'm good. I'm good."

Later, saying goodbye, they shook hands. Grady kept hold of Curt's for a minute. "You're thinking about paying a visit to Eli."

Curt didn't bother to deny it.

"Hold off awhile. Let me talk to him first."

Curt took his hand back. Brought a trembling cigarette to his mouth. "Never liked that guy much. Always thought he was maybe a little queer. All that poetry and shit."

"Just let me talk to him."

"You know well as me who did this."

"I got ideas, yeah. But ideas don't mean nothing. Put yourself in my shoes. Just hold off."

Curt coughed, spat. Handsome when he shaved and bathed, he didn't have a handsome man's confidence. It was an effort for him to look any man in the eye. He glanced downhill, considered the fresh mound of clay, the hillside that had only recently held his father. He'd driven past this spot ten thousand times. "Just how long? How long you expect me to hold off?"

Waking up on the third morning of her visit, taking the measure of her own humors, Chloe found anger, frustration, a bubbling, subsurface sob. She could have been in Yellowstone Park about now, maybe driving Montana's back roads, discovering saloons, cute little historical museums. Instead, Jesus, just look at her. Sweltering at six in the morning, staring up at a yellow fly strip clotted with gnats, moths.

Singer's poetry had emotion, energy, color, but she found the life behind that poetry curiously translucent. Thirty years spent inside this house. He said he'd been the youngest child and that made sense. He had a youngest-child's plaintive air about him.

She was not a religious person. Not for her, the bureaucracy of -isms. But she did believe in accountability. At the end of it, her final breath floating to the ceiling, there would be a reckoning. What had she done with the days she'd been given? Last year she spent her vacation in a stone farmhouse in the Dordogne, bought tins of *fois gras* at the Saturday market in Sarlat. The year before, she had stretched out under mosquito netting in Kruger, listened to lions roar beyond the walls. All that time, Singer had been here.

Yesterday, they'd herded cows. "We're shipping here in a week. You feel like helping me gather up some stragglers?"

She hadn't the first clue what he was talking about. But sure, why not.

Between her knees, a gentle, blaze-faced sorrel named Peaches. She whispered into a swiveling ear, "You and me are going places, honey." Put the odor of horses in her nostrils and she was ten years old again. Photos from that period show the last honest smiles of her childhood. She and Peaches followed Singer down into the Breaks, Dante and Beckett trotting on either side. Singer said, "They like to hole up at the head end of these coulees, up where it's cool." The sky hot and pale. Their horses drank deeply at a stock pond, then dug at the water with their hooves. The dogs lay flat in an inch of muddy water, panting. Singer circled, leaning over to study the ground. "These yearlings will leave a track not a whole lot different from a cow elk." In the timber, Chloe ducked for branches. Ahead of them five steers rolled to their feet, dull and astonished, then made a lumbering break for it. "Just let your horse there have her head. She knows what to do." Chloe's mare circled, shifted her weight, cut back and forth up the hill. Singer whistled to the dogs, pointing. The dogs flanked the steers, nipping. A few hours later, Chloe dismounted, rubbing her knees. "Is that the Fort Peck down there?" Ten, twelve times a day Singer would stop to scribble a note, a stub of a carpenter's pencil tight in his fist. Then he'd look around, briefly pleased. He ignored her question about Fort Peck (too obvious?), and she said, "Is that your little poetry notebook?"

He retreated to his Skoal can, thumping it hard with a forefinger. *Little*. "That's my little mind-your-own-business notebook."

He was attracted to her. Of course he was. His eyes went to her breasts, to her hips . . . but then, nada. All the normal gestures that preceded seduction—lingering touches, hands on shoulders, quick little neck massages—they were all absent. Did he think he was too old for her? It would be sweet if it weren't so frustrating. The gears that churn within men, the machinery that forces them after women? His were somehow all gummed up.

After a day in the saddle, woozy from wind and light and heat, she felt closer to him. He glanced at the Roman numeral count he'd written in pen on the palm of his hand, "Only three short. Pretty good day."

"What's for dinner there, Mr. Singer?"

Hamburgers, and a 1997 Stag's Leap Cabernet. He tasted the wine, raised his eyebrows. "Uh huh. I see it now. I mean, yeah." Bullshit, of course, but she appreciated the effort. They went to the couch. He had planned their first night's entertainment—his records—but hadn't thought so far as the second. "I got some old movies we could watch?" In a cabinet, dusty VHS versions of *Lethal Weapon*, Michael Keaton as Batman, *Shrek*. Everything you could get for five dollars at Walmart twenty years ago. She said, "How about we just sit and digest for a while."

Singer sat stiffly on the far side of the couch, as composed as a passenger on a train. "Weather guessers are saying we could get a little rain by the end of the week."

She slid closer to him. Gently extracted the wineglass from his fingers. He wouldn't meet her eyes. At this distance, she could see a burst vein within the curve of his nostril. She took his hand. This wasn't easy for her. Her fingertips on the knobs of his knuckles. *Don't talk*. She brought her other hand to his cheek. To the dark stubble going gray. She put a knuckle to his chin, and turned his face toward her. Just like that, easy as tripping down stairs, she kissed him.

But his lips stayed closed, and his breathing went shallow; a slight, controlled whistle through his nose. At least he had the good grace to leave the pulling away to her.

"Well." She sat back, nonplussed. "Well." She willed her eyes to fill with ice and ashes. "So. You're gay?"

He shook his head. "You really think this could work out, me and you? Montana, New York, back again? Not to mention, me being so much older?"

She took a few seconds. Okay, Chloe. Find the right tone, just the right word. "What the fuck, Singer."

"Eh now?" He'd already been congratulating himself for his level-headedness.

"You don't think we could work, but then, what? You were just, what, you were just waiting for me to make an ass out of myself before you mentioned it?"

"I just don't . . . Shit."

"Don't what."

"Look at you. How pretty." He took her hand. "Then look at me."

She was simultaneously offended and touched. What's the right play here? What's to be done. It took her only a second to decide. Don't hesitate, don't falter. They'd just opened another bottle of wine. She stood and bent for the bottle, letting him have a glimpse of freckled cleavage. "I'll be out on the porch."

He half stood, courteous to the end. "Chloe, listen, I'm . . ."

Kiss my ass and go fuck yourself. "Sleep well, Singer."

———

So, yeah. The next morning? I'm outta here.

She woke early. Padded softly through the house toward the shower. His yellow legal pad lay open on the kitchen table. She snuck a glance. Expecting poems, sketches, doodles, she found instead one long block of script. "Nature abhors not a vacuum but a line, a square. Every bristling, Euclidian porcupine eventually decomposes into a mound. The natural state resists corners. Entropy favors a circle. For a language to be more natural, shouldn't it aspire to this same geometry? This same shying away?" She'd hoped that he might have written something about her or her visit, but no. His last line referenced only William Stafford. "The light by the barn. More to be explored?" A few minutes later in the shower, she put her forehead against warm tile. Let the water run.

Coming out into the kitchen later, she heard the rattle of pans. Voices. Wrapped in a robe, drying her hair, she found a new face at the stove. "You must be Abe?" Short as a teenager, his skin was as wrinkled as a crumpled newspaper, as stained as a walnut. Singer's hired hand. He'd apparently been in Miles City paying a visit to his ninety-four-year-old mother. A little Jack Russell terrier lay in a corner of the kitchen, curled nose to tail, watching her alertly. Abe raised his spatula in a salute, grinning around a shelf of cheap dentures. "Eli said you were pretty, but he didn't say how pretty. I mean, damn."

Singer, at the table with his pad, was amused. "Good lord, Abe. Tell her what you really think, there."

"I aim to. Right after we introduce ourselves." He set the spatula aside to shake hands. "I'm Abe, and you're Chloe

Barnes from New York. How do you like your eggs there, Chloe from New York?" He assessed her hips, her breasts. If she'd been a watermelon, he'd already be knocking against her hull. She wasn't offended. Old men exist in their own netherworld of harmless flirtation.

Abe talked nonstop. Over her eggs ("Fried, thanks"), she learned that he tended the farm's chickens and butchered the pigs. "So I cook the breakfast, ain't that right, Eli." He scratched at an ancient corrugation of razor burn around his wattled neck. "Had me two wives, hosted two funerals. Second wife died in childbirth. Lost the baby, too." He said this matter-of-factly, without self-pity. "And now it's just me and Eli here. Running the place. Just enough ranch to starve on, ain't it, Eli?" Cowboys, both of them. The real deal.

She touched the corners of her mouth with a paper towel napkin. "When can you drive me back to Billings, Singer?"

Singer was studying his coffee. Raising it to his lips, he held her gaze, but it cost him something. "I was hoping you might stay awhile longer."

"I don't see how."

Abe glanced back and forth between them, catching up.

"Just a day or two, maybe. I was thinking you could ride Peaches out again. Explore a little on your own. Give her a workout for me. It would be a favor."

Christ, Singer. Apology meets pleading puppy. She felt a flare of power. Whatever vulnerability she'd shown by coming here, whatever measure of pride had been sacrificed by walking off that plane, things were realigning in her favor. She smelled regret, a soupçon of self-flagellation. And besides: When would she have a chance to ride a horse again?

"What do you think Abe," she said. "Should I go for a ride?"

She had her own agenda. Of course she did. Did Singer think he could just buy her off with a horseback ride? Think again, mister. During their ride yesterday, he had pointed out Abe's trailer. A hunched-up antique camper settled low on four flat tires. Abe ate his lunch alone, apparently. Part of his daily routine. Breakfast with Singer, dinner with Singer, but lunch and a nap back at his trailer. If she left Singer's around ten or so, circled to the south, came around from the north, she should catch the old guy by himself.

Despite the heat, a thread of smoke rose from the stovepipe. Paths in the grass, parking pad to door. She dismounted and wrapped reins loose around a bumper. Knocked flimsy tin. "Anybody home?" The door's aluminum handle had been repaired with a cracked porcelain knob.

Shrill barking sounded from inside, followed by a pot clattering on a stove. "Yeah, hello there. Just a minute." The door opened. "Chloe?" He held his dog away from the door with his heel. "Help you with something?"

"Mind if I come in?"

"Um." Abe glanced around his trailer, half-panicked. "Give me a second?"

"Sorry for just barging in."

"Just give me a second." He closed the door, left her standing on the stoop. Inside, the sound of cabinet doors, a rattle of a shower curtain. Five minutes later, Abe was back in the door, saying, "Get you a cup of tea or some such?"

"Sorry to barge." She stepped past him into the trailer, noting the bath towel thrown over a sink full of dirty dishes. The wet trail of a dishcloth still glistening across his counter. A wood stove, metal coffee pot blackened on the bottom. A combination shower and restroom filled with hanging shirts. A coil of rope hung from the back of her chair. A not unpleasant smell of dogs and aged body, a sharp tang of disinfectant.

She'd imposed on him. But this thing with Singer. She had questions.

"You got to understand about Eli, I never seen a man so determined about doing the right thing." Abe had his mug of hot tea and was squeezing in a thread of honey. "I've known him, what, thirty years now. I ain't *never* caught him in a lie. You think about that for a minute. How many folks you know never lie? It ain't natural, is what I'm saying. But that's Eli Singer."

"*Everybody* lies."

"You'd think so, but no. Reason I mention it, I saw how you and him were locking horns this morning, and normally I'd say I don't blame you."

"Oh?"

"You heard about how Eli must be the one sending Curt Fahler all that cash, all these years now. Hell I was down in Miles City and I heard about it all the way down there. Well, just yesterday, I come right out and asked him, I said, You got any notion about how Pete Fahler came to be buried on our place? He said, Abe, he said, I don't know the first thing about it. And you bet, sure, yeah, I believe him. Thirty years."

"Where would I have heard about Curt Fahler's cash money?"

He sipped tea, nonplussed. "So what's happened between you two?"

She came back with a question of her own. "Cash money?" Tried to give it an incidental, just-passing-the-time kind of vibe. A literary agent, she had a nose for a story. For a compelling question with complications. "Curt Fahler's, what, Pete Fahler's son?"

Abe was a gossip to the bone. Knew he shouldn't, but: "After Pete disappeared, these envelopes full of cash started showing up in the mailbox." A fake regret at the absurdity of it. "First they went to Curt's mother, then after Curt got married, they went to him and his wife. Hundred here, three or four hundred there. Whole county knew about it. We all figured, hell, Pete's shacked up with some chippy somewheres. Feels guilty, wants to make amends. This went on for years."

"And now it turns out that, what, Pete was buried on Singer's ranch? All this time, right?"

"Right. So who's been sending Curt the cash? That's the thousand-dollar question. What everybody's been chewing over."

"Singer says he doesn't know anything about it?"

"And I believe him. I do. Thirty years, never told a lie."

Chloe thought: Bullshit. But was kind enough to let it go unsaid. Let the old man keep his illusions. "Thank you for the tea."

"You don't have to run off so soon?"

"Singer will be wondering where I got to."

"He couldn't talk about nothing else before you got here. You should know that. Two solid weeks, it was Chloe this,

Chloe that. He'd ask me, you think she'd like to go for a ride? You think she'd like steaks for dinner? Pain in the ass about it, you want the truth."

"Well." Don't be touched, Chloe. Don't be swayed. "Anyway. I should get back."

She already knew his rituals. Lying in bed, she listened to a brief spray of dishwater into the sink, the mechanical turn of a key into the grandfather clock. He brushed his teeth, spat. When she heard the toilet flush for the last time, she slipped into her robe.

She walked past the dogs asleep on the couch. His bedroom door was cracked. She pressed it open with her palm. "Singer?" He lay in the dark, facing away. In the wedge of light allowed by the door, here was his bare back, salted with a handful of flesh-colored moles. He twisted around, one arm raised against the new light. Such a white torso. She said, "I can't sleep."

After a long moment—she breathed, then breathed again, then sighed through her nose—he raised a corner of his bedcover, opening it for her.

They carried breakfast plates around each other with slow, coordinated courtesy. He said, "Excuse me, love." *Love*, he'd said.

The sex? Decent, but not exceptional. Twelve, fifteen minutes. And he brought nothing new to the postgame. She wasn't disappointed, not exactly. It was just . . .

They talked tattoos. Not that she wasn't proud of her ink (expensive, Smith Street), but she wasn't used to giving it more than a few minutes. She had Vonnegut around her ankle ("So it Goes") and Rilke down her back. Roethke inside her thigh ("The greatest assassin of life is haste") and Valérie on her calf. Singer traced Roethke with a fingertip. "He was Hugo's mentor. You knew that, right?"

"What about you, Singer?"

"Me? I got no tattoos. Scars, no tattoos." He fell back into his pillow.

"What about you and Curt Fahler." Entitled by sex, she felt she could risk it.

He opened an eye. "Where'd you hear about Curt Fahler?"

"Around."

"You shouldn't listen to every goddamn rumor comes down the pike."

"Methinks he doth protest too much." And she did. A guy gets pissed ten minutes after he gets laid? Either he's ashamed and hiding it, or embarrassed and dodging a bullet. If she'd been a guard dog, one lip would be curling up.

Maybe if she'd had a month in Montana, even another week, they might have had time to let this—whatever this was—settle into some kind of understandable shape and form. Was it a prelude to something larger? Or was it just a polite diversion. But they didn't have a week. And so she found herself dwelling less on the possibilities and more on the potential catastrophes. The complications. What was the backstory?

The day before she was due to fly home, the Garfield County Sheriff came by for an interview. Singer led him into the kitchen. "Grady? This here's Chloe. Chloe's visiting from back east."

When the sheriff lifted his square-crowned hat, a slab of carefully manufactured combover rose with it. He couldn't have been more than thirty-five or so. Bummer to be going bald so young. A thick, reddish-gray mustache hid his lips. "Ma'am," he said, and seemed reluctant to shake her hand. The way he tucked his khaki uniform blouse into his jeans said *amateur*, but then your eye went to the badge, the pistol. He looked around the kitchen with bland, sleepy-eyed curiosity. So many books. He nodded in her general direction. Said to Singer, "So I was hoping you and me and Abe could talk private. Apologies, ma'am."

"That's fine," Chloe stood. "Excuse me, I have manuscripts to read."

She retreated to the porch. A redwood chair splintering on the legs and arms. Drawn to the sound of the screen door, the dogs loped around the side of the house, pushed their heavy heads under her hand, eased down with theatrical sighs. The kitchen windows were open behind her. Had she planned it this way? Maybe, maybe. In any case, without trying particularly hard, she was able to catch most of the conversation, the high points, everything but words lowered out of inadvertent propriety.

Grady's tone was slow, reasonable. He was careful of his phrasing. Laying out a case. "So yeah, Eli. You can see why folks would think Buddy's some kind of a suspect. Only suspect, really. A body shows up on your place, and given Pete's history with this family, with Buddy . . . I mean, you can understand it, yeah?"

"I understand it. Doesn't mean I agree with it."

"Plus, I mean, you see how this all reflects on you. Much as I hate to say it, who's been sending money to Curt all these years? Has to be Eli Singer. Which means you've had to have known about it, been in on it. You're complicit. I'm being honest with you now. But that's the skinny around Jordan."

"You got it all wrong, see I . . ."

Abe interrupted. "So is this what the taxpayers of our county are paying you for, Grady?" Abe let his voice rise. "Come out here and harass hard-working citizens? I remember when you were poaching elk in August for velvet. You didn't think I knew about that, did you? Well I did, and so did a lot of other people. I know everything goes on in this county, and I'm telling you you're wasting your goddamn time out here."

"All right then, Abe. Goddamnit yourself. You tell me who I should be interviewing. I'll go pay them a visit."

"How about Pete's widow over in Glasgow. If there was anybody ever had a reason to put a bullet into that lying sonofabitch, it was that poor woman."

"So then she started sending cash to herself, then her own kid? Think about that for a second."

Abe harrumphed. "That ain't no kind of argument. There's always some kind of other explanation."

"Yeah, uh huh. What is it, then?"

"So now you want me to do your job for you?"

Chloe's manuscript lay forgotten on her lap. Singer, an accessory. How much did it matter to her? She dropped a stone into the dark well of her own temperament. Waited for a splash. Was still waiting. He'd been twelve. And even if true, you could see how a guy might get caught up in his own evasion. At some point it would be too late. But then again, imagine what it would do to you. Living with it. Those icebergs of guilt.

What *did* matter to her—naturally enough—was the story behind the evasion. What had happened here? She found herself fascinated. All the way out here in godforsaken Montana, a tiny little melodrama. And where did it put her vis-à-vis Singer? Was she just another dupe? Another one of the clueless over which he's pulling some wool? The thing about liars, even the good ones, there's always an element of scorn, of smugness. You fools, was the subtext. Was she a fool?

She'd be damned if she was.

Twenty minutes later, Chloe came around the house to find the three of them standing by Grady's truck. Grady had his hands in his hip pockets and was twisting at his lower back, stretching, wincing, squinting at clouds. "You should have my job for a day, Eli. I swear. I sent old Pete to the crime lab in Missoula? They're telling me about how much they don't like my excavation. I mean, how are you supposed to dig up a dead guy? Then I got newspapers calling from all over. Connecticut, Detroit. Places you didn't know even had papers. This thing's drawing some kind of attention, I'll tell you what. Miserable job. Anyway, Chloe, real pleased to meet you."

"You too."

Grady climbed into his truck. Rolled down his window, said to Singer, "I hear you're shipping steers this week?"

"Thursday."

It seemed to satisfy Grady in some oblique way, that the business of the world was still ticking along, as if only at his sufferance. "Well, all right then."

They left the ranch in a gray and grainy dawn. As Singer drove, she had a privileged view to the end of the night. A raccoon rolled along chubby and quick through the barrow pit. A mule deer doe grazed toward the timber, two fawns beside her. Topping out onto flat farm ground, a pheasant sprinted smoothly across the road. She said, "If anybody around here ever gives your poetry a good close read, they're going to have some serious questions about that guy Pete Fahler."

"What do you mean?"

"A lot of bones in there. A lot of blood crying from the ground."

"Biblical imagery."

"But you can see how people might get the wrong idea."

"Don't you start in on me now."

"What about this guy, this Buddy? You think he had something to do with it?" She found herself avoiding the word *murder*. "I mean, you were a kid. You couldn't have been with him *all* the time." Even in her current mood—conflicting emotions: vulnerability, frustration (she'd let herself *fall* for the guy)—she didn't want to press too hard. But.

"Where'd you hear about Buddy?"

"You and Grady talked with the window open." She refused to be embarrassed. "Anyway, what about him."

"Not Buddy, no."

"Who did it then?"

He shook his head. "Everybody's looking at me like I got answers." He studied her. "I'm feeling put upon, you want the truth."

"So you're not going to talk to me?"

"I got nothing to say."

"You've never really told me anything about yourself. Nothing real, nothing personal."

"Not all that much to talk about."

"Awful way to go through life, you ask me."

"How's that?"

"Not trusting anyone."

He pursed his lips.

"What."

"Nothing."

"Let me tell you something, Singer. I know you better than you think I do."

"Doubt it."

"I can read you like a goddamned book. You've been wondering, what's she even *doing* here? Is she trying to trap me or something? Then you turn around and think, no, she's like a gift, one last chance to have a normal life. One minute you're afraid of me, next minute you're thinking wedding bells."

"Well."

"I'm the best goddamn thing that ever happened to you. You're just too dumb to see it."

He was quiet for a time. Then, "I get along."

"What's that supposed to mean?"

"I'll keep on getting along. That's what I do."

In an early poem, he talked about the unearned arrogance of ranchers, the flippant, cocksure dismissal of opinions contrary to their own. The kind of arrogance that arises from ignorance. The entitled who haven't been knocked around enough to understand their own fallibility. Chloe's opinion? Singer had the same kind of problem. "I don't even know what to say to that." Her feelings were hurt, which pissed her off. How had they already gotten to a place where he was capable of hurting her? Fuck him.

In the Billings airport, she gave him a one-armed hug goodbye, willing him to think of his empty dresser at home, the surface clear of cosmetics and hairpins, a strategically forgotten tube of hair conditioner on the tub. She put her lips close to his ear. "You're going to miss me so fucking much."

Buddy

As a boy he'd toddled behind a plow
burying seeds with his feet, a sweep and a stamp.
His people weren't much for talking but

took the time to say that God's first purpose
is to receive our gratitude. He squeezed a
morning udder, climbed trees to knock at apples.

The world was flat and the sun flew
around and the only news worth hearing
was in next Sunday's sermon.

My people: Their children died like stones
skipped across water, their teeth wobbled loose and
every day they awoke whispering thank you, thank you.
If only to themselves.

AT SOME POINT YOU stop trying to triumph and content yourself with simply persisting. Any man with half a brain should go maudlin over a woman who consents to sleep with him. At one point, she'd asked me about Abe—"Is he good with horses?"—and, maybe out of nervousness, I answered too well. "He has this old buckskin gelding named Moses. Once every couple days, Abe will give Mo a once-over. Understand now he probably should have put this horse down five years ago. But here's Abe out there proud as a teenager waxing his hot rod. He climbs through the fence and they just start walking toward each other, meeting about halfway. That man's got the gentlest heart of anybody I ever met, is what I'm saying."

Yesterday, Abe suggested our freezer could use some meat. "I'll lend a hand, you want to go put one on the ground." A concession on his part. He generally scorns bow hunting—"That stick and string"—but he's been worried about me. Anyway, it was true that we needed the meat. I kept my old compound in the shed, hanging from a weathered antler. Broadheads in an old cigar box. If there is such a thing as sin in this world it lies in ignoring a Montana fall, in letting the sun rise unremarked over frost-limned hay bales, in failing to hear at least one elk bugle.

Five-thirty in the morning, I found Abe waiting on his

stoop, an old camo jacket buttoned to his chin, Ruthie shivering on his lap. He's gone through a series of these lapdogs. The saddest twenty-square-inches in Montana? A bureau drawer filled with his collection of leather dog collars. "When I get to finally meet god," he has said, "first question I'm asking is how come he made dogs get old so much quicker than people. It's just cruel, you ask me. Cruel." Like Buddy, I favor heelers and shepherds, dogs that work. But I've envied Abe's rapport with his lapdogs. He told me once, "I'd never keep a dog who'd vote Democrat."

He whispered now, "They been bugling all night, just on the south end of that school section. We been keeping track, haven't we, Ruthie?"

A slight breeze blew into our faces. "Temperature's dropping. Snow's coming."

An elk bugled down in the distant dark. Quarter mile away, at the most. A long, rising whistle then a quick drop into grunts. Two more bulls answered. We had a herd, then. "Let's circle around, maybe walk up on them from below."

I've branded cows with Abe, dug fence posts, strung wire and fought fires, discussed horse and cattle breeding, argued my atheism against his shopworn dogma, and yet it still seems odd that my closest friend should be this crass, benignly racist old man. World War II gave him a limp and some firm ideas about Japanese car manufacturers. He respects my time in Iraq, not knowing I enlisted only as a final, failed effort to leave Garfield County behind. My poetry puts a puzzled little coda between his eyes and my weakness for red wine tickles him. He likes it that I have such a visible flaw. If I sleep past six o'clock, he'll say, "You take communion again last night?"

Abe doesn't deny the machinery of the world, nature red in tooth and claw, but would prefer not to have the blood on his own hands. His insistence on cooking our breakfasts (poking at the home-smoked bacon sputtering in a pan, whisking the eggs into a scramble) is a kind of penance. He sees it as a failing that he is a creature among creatures.

Four hours later, we sat together above my bull elk. *My* bull now. It lay askew in dead branches, head twisted back, the thick black hair of its stomach conveniently exposed for my knife. Small spits of snow blew sideways, collecting in its hair, one cold eye. I did not write the rules but I can acknowledge them. Abe blew his nose into his handkerchief. I hit my knife on the whetstone. Tested it on my forearm. Abraham, who knows me as well as anyone, said, "She reminded me some of your sister."

Even at fourteen, Emma had been the sort of girl who, to borrow a line from Bukowski, might have once been burned at the stake. Before coming to the ranch, we had been united by concern for our mother, by our shared poverty. We had little to call our own. Clothes, my paper route, Emma's babysitting gigs. We sat together on the porch, feeling the hot wind, listening to the kind of bone-deep silence that, until then, had existed only in libraries. Anger came off of her in waves. "Just look at it. Jesus." Chickens scratched in the yard and a pair of coarse-haired goats tugged at weeds, bells around their necks clanging.

That night we lay awake under a single sheet. Through the window, the burp of toads from the reservoir, the cries of nameless birds. There was a scratching on the roof, claws against tin. Emma whispered, "It's just an owl. Just an owl." Our knees touched. She hissed, "Keep on your side." In the kitchen, Buddy cleared his throat and shifted in his chair. Mother sipped from her glass, coughed, then sipped again. "Well, that's an original kind of taste."

"Work-a-day's end," Buddy said. "Momma and I would take a glass or two of chokecherry wine. Especially if there was something to celebrate. Birthday, or whatnot."

I whispered, "What's a chokecherry?"

Emma held a finger to her lips.

"So here's to new friends. Cheers."

Glasses clinked. Mother was surely staring and trying not to stare at this enormous stranger, this man to whom she had committed herself and her two children. The commitment was perhaps not irrevocable, but it felt that way. Four hours to the south in Billings, the gears of our old life were still ticking happily along. We had known our street signs, the sound of Mr. Volker's mower from next door, the brown patches in our lawn that would never ever flourish. Gone now. Even if we left this ranch, where would we go?

The pauses in their conversation grew awkward. Buddy said again, probably raising his glass to the portrait on the wall, "Wish you could have met my momma."

My mother said, "Is that a fiddle up on the mantel there?"

"You like a fiddle? You like fiddle music?"

"Do you play?" Her voice had gone overly bright, the voice she used as she tried (and invariably failed) to hold onto a good mood. If previous patterns held true, the next few days would find her irritable. Then mute and hollow. Despondent.

She would get one of her headaches, and sprawl across the floor, damp rag over her eyes.

Heavy feet creaked on boards. Mother whispered in the tones of conspiracy, "Not very loud, though."

He didn't play the dance number you might have expected, no schottische or reel. "I call this one 'November Moon.'" A simple melody, it contained within it the tweet of birds, the squeal of dying rabbits. A slow, mournful exploration of the scale. It was beautiful. Remembering it now, I think of Philip Glass. I would later watch him play similar tunes with his fiddle butted up against his bicep rather than held under his chin, wearing a look of such concentration that it bordered on anger, his gentle, heavy-skinned face twisted into scowls and sneers. It was a long piece, and ten minutes later, as he let the final note fall away, Mother said (her voice gone soft and surprised and sincere), "Buddy, oh my. That was just lovely."

Under the sheet, my sister took my hand.

Buddy said, "I just enjoy a fiddle now and then." We heard him clip it back into its case. "You play any instruments?"

"No, not really."

"Momma always said everybody should play something or another."

"Well, I used to play the piano a little bit. Emma too. She was taking lessons."

"What happened?"

"We went through a tight pinch, and well . . ." She cleared her throat.

He eased back into his chair. "I've always thought a piano would sound good around here. It's a piano-playing kind of house, don't you think?"

He had come to Garfield County as a child, the youngest of three children. Ten years old in the fall of 1941. They drove from Iowa in the family's International pickup, the kids dusty in the bed, playing paper-rock-scissors, spitting between their bare feet, dozing elbow to elbow. On the cusp of war, the tail end of a depression, they pulled their meager furnishings (bureau, bed, grandfather clock) behind them on a flatbed trailer, exposed to the wind and rain; lashed with clotheslines. The transmission began to grumble in Jordan, second and third gear packed it in around Devil's Creek, and by the time they coasted up in front of the one-room cabin, the radiator was hissing out a white plume, the tailgate hung on by a single hinge, and a front tire wobbled like a dropped plate. Their father, the wayward son of a minister, unbuttoned his drawers and splattered urine up and down the front door. "I christen thee Rattletrap Ranch!"

Ahead of them still, the full and dwindling play of their lives. World War II took the eldest son, Manny, calling him off to the Pacific with two changes of clothes and a dishtowel full of cinnamon rolls. He died either on the death march (according to a letter from his colonel) or of dysentery in the days before (one of his bunkmates). Five years later, the father passed away painfully with a snapped spine, courtesy of a green-broke colt. Buddy found him with his fingernails furrowed into the ground. Birds had been at his eyes. A full ten years after that, Buddy's unmarried sister Yvonne died by her own hand on a sandstone bluff above Wolfpen. Their father's pistol in her mouth, a dusting of blood across the sage and cheat grass. Suicide is to the Breaks what smallpox was to the Indians. Although he never spoke of it, it had to be that Buddy, who rode past this place often, was compelled to dwell on the circumstances of this, his favorite sibling's, death. The black-eyed smile that had picked a banjo to his fiddle.

Buddy and his mother were left alone, stewing, squabbling slow through the same old arguments, molding themselves into each other the way trees bulge around barbed wire. She cut his hair and patched his pants, cooked his meals and hung his laundry, corrected *lay* for *lie* and *ain't* for *isn't*. Her portrait? Stern and judgmental, a pearl brooch at her neck and steel-gray hair braided in loops around her ears. "Whenever I start feeling sorry for myself," he told me once, "I think about Momma, about how she always kept her chin up, looked on the bright side." Erroll Morris, however, neighbor three places to the west, told me, "Awful woman, I mean just *awful*. Bitch under a bonnet. My missus would now and then take over a plate of something or other, maybe a pot of some of that good stew she makes, and Sally Singer would lift up the lid and sniff and say about how she didn't accept charity, especially when it had too much pepper in it."

A few years before her death, Buddy took his mother to a pie social. He'd been invited the play fiddle with the band, and his mother came along to be censorious. She sat off to one side with her best (and only) friend, Alma Whittaker. An hour into it, Buddy stepped away to have a sip of punch. To his astonishment, the new schoolteacher in Jordan wove her way through the room to ask him for a dance. Erroll told me, "Ugly as ten miles of mud fence, but a sweet woman. Hard worker. Would have been a perfect match." A heavy brow and a wattle, but bold enough to show him her hand, wait for him to reach out and shake it. "Pauline. Care to swing me around the floor a few numbers?" Buddy swallowed, then nodded emphatically. They waltzed stiffly together for five minutes, maybe ten, before Buddy noted the glower around his mother. "Guess that band needs their fiddle back." Pauline showed him her crooked teeth, and stretched to kiss him on the cheek. "Thank you for the dances there, Mister Singer."

For a schoolteacher, it was a bold gesture. Not like getting drunk at Hell Creek Bar, but enough to make the gossips raise their eyebrows. Driving home, his momma sat twisting at the straps of her purse. She stretched them tight, snapped them like a garrote. "Can you believe that little hussy coming up to you just out of the blue like that? Women these days, I swear. And a schoolteacher!"

"She seemed nice."

"Oh ho! Nice, did she? Well, let me tell you about nice . . ."

Later that week, Buddy heard his mother pick up the phone. "Well, let me just see if he's in . . . ," a pause; then, "Can I have him call you back?"

"Who was that, Momma?"

"Nobody worth knowing."

Years to come, when he thought about women, he thought about Pauline. Planting winter wheat, rumbling slow around a field, twisting to study the shivering slide of seed through his drill, he could smell her perfume, feel the slick silk fabric of her blouse, her hardwood-girdled waist under his hand. Evenings, after dinner, he scratched his fiddle while Momma knitted or sewed or churned. Later, he read aloud from Emerson, Thoreau, the Encyclæpedia Britannica.

"Here's something, Momma. That Great Wall in China? Says here it's really a whole series of walls."

Sally Singer rocked over her knitting. "I've always wondered why folks didn't just go get some ladders."

"I've been thinking I should get in touch with that Pauline."

She yanked yarn from its basket. "Little miss hussy? You can do better."

"Well, maybe I should call her up."

"One of these days, you'll find a woman who'll see you for what you are."

"That's okay, Momma. I was just thinking out loud. But yeah, no, that's okay."

His mother's breasts were taken one and then the other. Her final words, waving a skeletal hand toward the open window, were something about oranges, how she smelled oranges. He was left alone, paging at night through his tattered scrapbook, scribbling incidental remembrances. Who was there to care about the details of his day? The magazines he took in the mail, the ball joint he'd just replaced, the killdeer faking a broken wing in the yard. His days became ephemeral, translucent. He frayed at the edges. He was unsurprised when doors closed of their own accord, when footsteps creaked across the floor of the next room. He spoke to the empty room. "You having a good day today, Momma?"

From the first, Emma wanted nothing more than to pry us away from Buddy, from his ranch. Expulsion or rejection, it didn't matter; she was desperate only to be someplace else, someplace not here.

I woke to sound of chickens chuckling under the eaves. Across the room, Emma had taken a tiny mirror (shoplifted from MiniMart) and hung it from a stray nail beside the closet. She wore jeans rolled at the cuff, a blouse tied in a knot below her breasts. She stood close to the mirror, twisting, scowling. She sprayed Aquanet and shook her head emphatically. I'd seen the ritual five thousand times before. Usually it was done with self-indulgence, pleasure. But now she was impatient, short-tempered, jerking her fingers through a tangle. Even if she achieved that rare, once-a-year balance of self-image and reality, there would be no one around her now with the expertise to appreciate it. "You'd better get up and get moving. I can hear that Buddy clumping around out there."

"Why should I care?" I still had only the vaguest notions of what might be expected from me (although the words "especially boys" carried ominous overtones).

"You didn't hear him last night? He wants to, quote, *introduce you to the place*, unquote. God, where did he come from? Can you imagine?"

Buddy's voice rose from the kitchen, querulous as a child. "Momma always cut apples up into my oatmeal, Miss Donahue."

"Find me some apples, I'll cut them up for you."

Buddy could lift a railroad tie to his shoulder. His fingers were knobby as truck tires. Black hair peppered his wrists. He knew how to sew up a heifer's prolapsed uterus, build a log cabin. But the social two-step of favor and obligation was a mystery to him. "Guess I'm not too hungry after all."

"Suit yourself."

This was not a promising start.

Ten minutes later, I found Mother standing alone in the middle of the kitchen. "Just *look* at this place. I mean, *look* at it." A cleaning rag limp in her hands, a plastic bucket empty beside her. A bottle of Lysol, a brush. She tucked a strand of hair behind her hair. "You need to get your little butt outside. He's waiting for you."

I found a blue Chevy Blazer newly parked by the corral. With no fenders and side mirrors, it had a narrow, unstable look. A pair of horses stood saddled beside it, noses buried in grain boxes. Buddy stood talking to a man in his early forties. "Eli? This here's Abe. Roustabout on the place. Abe? This here's Eli Singer."

Abe was skinny and pale, slight as a housecat. Hair the consistency of dandelion fluff. His skin close to albino, he had a chapped look around the eyes and mouth and an open, eager expression which I found appealing.

"Pleased to meet you, sir."

Buddy grinned. "Always knew you were a *sir* there, Abe."

Abe shook my hand with a one-two pump. "You just call me Abe." Despite the heat, he wore long johns under his overalls, a gray, long-sleeved shirt buttoned to the neck.

"Abe here's mucking out stalls before it gets too hot. Me and you are going for a ride. You been on a horse before? Okay. Don't matter one way or the other. I train gentle horses. We'll go for a ride, check some fences, I'll show you around the place."

He held my horse for me. Within ten minutes, we were riding. Twenty yards to the ground, and my horse swayed like a teeter-totter. If this was being a cowboy, I wasn't sure I cared for it. We followed a ranch road. Meadowlarks flushed away, bobbing. Buddy discussed—without segue or context—the French penchant for eating songbirds, his theories on how electricity gives you headaches, and the New Deal. He mentioned the Judiths and the Little Rockies. "There's a town in the Little Rockies, Landusky? I guess Pike Landusky used to ride with Butch Cassidy." A small plane buzzed overhead. Without looking up he said, "That's old man Dutton. He flies out of Sand Springs." Buddy hupped his horse down a shoulder of hillside, the trail not quite as wide as two hooves set side to side. It seemed to me a dangerous and unlikely descent. At one point, on the western edge of the property, we dismounted, hunkered over his heels. "I come up here now and then, thinking about my old dad. He'd tell stories about the Indians, Gros Ventre and Blackfeet, riding through all painted up. Or the homesteaders, how they just scratched all day long at bedbugs. Bedbugs was a plague back then."

"What came next. After the homesteaders?"

He was pleased by my curiosity. "Well that was my old dad."

"And now there's us, right?"

"Sure, you bet. Now there's us." He had been sifting through a handful of clay and gravel, tossing it palm to palm. And now he pinched up a shard of slate broken in the shape of a fish. "Look it here how pretty." He spat on it and wiped it clean, held it out for me. "You put that in your pocket. Something to remember the day by. Our first ride together. Tomorrow we'll take us a real ride. I got some yearlings on gain down in Cherry Creek. Them yearlings always get into trouble." He held my stirrup for me. "Figured I'd pay you about like them old-time waddies. Once a month. Five hundred suit you okay?"

"Five hundred *dollars?*"

"Sure." He dug his thick fingertips around in a can of Copenhagen, nodding at the westernmost fence. "Over there on that other side, bank took that ground for taxes. Guy named Pete Fahler? Pete owns it now. I tried to sell it to him market value but he claimed he was broke. Then the sonofabitch went and bought it cheap off the bank." He spat, and climbed into the saddle. Reined his horse around hard. "You ever get it in mind to play with matches, you play with them over this way. You hear me?"

I found Mother in the mudroom, scrubbing linoleum, face hidden behind a screen of stale, kinked hair. "Don't even *think* about coming in this house with those boots on." During her rare cleaning days in Billings, she would sip a beer while she pushed the vacuum. Lackadaisical, disinterested. This was a new Mother, one I'd never seen before. She'd thrown Buddy's windows open, tumbled the drapes in a pile on the floor; a washing machine chugged somewhere in the back, shaking the walls. A garbage can was filled with spoiled food from the fridge. The odor had changed. It smelled like a mother working. I said, "Can I help?"

"Heck yeah." She handed me a rag and a bottle of Windex. "Do what you can." She made a helpless gesture. "I mean, *try.*"

Ten minutes later, I stood out in the yard looking through the window to our room. The inside pane was open. I stood on an overturned bucket and sprayed Windex. Said through the screen, "What are you reading?"

Emma lay on our bed, kicking her bare heels. She had taken down the framed needlepoints and taped up, in their place, posters of Elton John, David Cassidy, Don Henley. "*Rolling Stone.*" She primly turned a page. "Mom wanted me to do that. Wash windows."

"Oh?"

"I told her this wasn't my house. That's just what I said. Not my house."

"What'd she say?"

"Oh. You know." She turned a page. "He collects things."

"Buddy?"

"Yeah. Little rocks, dried-up old flowers. Scattered all over the place. In his dresser? With his underwear? Mom found a bunch of spaghetti noodles all shriveled up. You know what the tag said? 'Momma's last meal.'"

"Some people *like* their mothers."

"I tried to take a bath? There wasn't any hot water."

"Not ever?"

"He's got an old hot water tank that burns wood. I didn't even know there was such a thing. And that cook stove he's got? That burns wood too. And there's no dryer. He's got a brand new washer, but no dryer."

"It'll be like the old days. Like you read about. It'll be fun."

"Yeah," she snorted, "for about five seconds. I told Mom, I said, 'If you think I'm going to scrub out somebody else's shitter you've got another . . .'"

"You're mean."

"What?"

"You're being *mean*."

She rested her chin on the heel of her palm. "You don't know every little thing, Eli."

"He really wants us to like him."

She flipped a page. "Tough titties."

He spent his days with cows, but he didn't necessarily care for them. When he spoke to them, which was often, it was in frustrated vulgarities, shouted epithets. "Get in there you sonofabitch. Goddamned blow bag piece of shit." He tolerated them the way electricians tolerate electricity, doctors and disease. Cows were a necessity but they weren't the reason.

I knew he was alone, but I hadn't realized the depth of his isolation until he held his spring branding. The slight smirks from cowboys younger than Buddy, the patronizing pats from matronly old women. He was a man who lived under the burden of sneers. He was a communal sacrifice made by those who need another's misery, another's isolation, in order to feel valued, to feel as if they belong.

He'd given me a set of work clothes from his own childhood. A western-cut shirt and a pair of patched jeans rolled at the cuff. Broken cowboy boots two sizes too large (I filled them with paper towels, toe and heel), and a foam and mesh baseball cap advertising seed. I sat on fence poles watching muddy ranch trucks file into Buddy's yard. Wives reached back for Lucite platters of casserole. The men gravitated toward the fires inside the corral, branding irons levered into the coals. I fidgeted. I sat. I stood rocking on the lowest rung of the fence. I checked my zipper. I had the sense of ritual. A gathering of the capable and self-assured. This was the tending to of the beasts. A ceremony. An old one. Ancient, maybe.

Behind the house, Mother stood over Buddy's grill. A tendril of smoke rose over the roof. Beside me, Emma had a strand of hay ironically in her lips. She'd taken her least-favorite pair of jeans and cut them short; tiny, white flags of pockets showed at the hips. As each ranch truck emptied out, she whispered nicknames in my ear. "Look at those two. Ozzie and Harriet meet Bert and Ernie. Bozzie and Hernia." Out of boredom (I thought), she eventually circulated through the crowd. Smiling, touching arms, she gave and received compliments. I thought her very adult. Slim as a heron.

Inside the pen, Buddy and Abe separated calves from cows. The calves stood huddled together in a knot at the far end of the enclosure. One fence over, the mother cows lowed hard. Buddy mounted his horse and stepped it forward, rope open and swinging. The first calf was roped and drug backward. Two other men whom I didn't know held the calf to the dirt, loosening the rope. A syringe full of vaccine went into its hip, horn clippers released a squirt of blood. Balls were squeezed out through a slit in the scrotum and tossed in a bucket.

Off my elbow, a voice said, "You wouldn't think somebody so plug ugly would be able to throw such a pretty loop." I glanced up for the first time at Pete Fahler.

In his late forties, Pete's skin was the color of weak tea. He wore a new black Resistol hat, and under the hat, a graying-black flourish of hair, a well-oiled pompadour. "I hear you're Buddy's new cowboy around the place. Somebody said the name Eli?"

I squinted enough to show suspicion. Who was this guy to call Buddy ugly? I'd made my allegiances. "Yeah. Eli."

He put a cigarette in his lips to shake my hand, forefinger missing at the first knuckle. To amuse children, I would later (and often) see him stick this stump deep into one nostril. "Now me," he said, "I credit it to that rope he's using. Nice little rawhide lariat. Wove it up for him when he wasn't much bigger than you are now. You won't find many people anymore can weave those good rawhide ropes. But me, I'm one of them."

"Okay."

"Yup, braid a rope, break a horse, I'm head to tail the real cowboy deal, the last gen-you-wine artifact. If I was in a museum, city folks would pay money for a glimpse."

"Are you the guy who stole that chunk of property from Buddy?" I surprised myself like this from time to time, letting loose a flare of insult.

Pete spat between his toes, showed me the top of his hat. A moment later, he tilted up a lopsided grin. "Well, I'd best get on, boy. Bulls to steers." He showed me his pocketknife, the lock-blade Buck. He opened it in front of my nose. Blood dried in the crevices. "There's some nutcutters in this crowd but I'm the cuttinest one of em all."

Emma came back, slurping a Diet Coke.

I said, "What's got you looking like a cat that ate a canary?"

"Just having fun, that's all. Talking to all these nice, nice people."

"Ohhkay." Thinking: Oh shit. Emma?

A flash-fire of hair around a branding iron, a bawl, a bleat. Flies buzzed. Mother emerged wearing a pretty blue dimity dress. From his horse, Buddy glanced at her, then glanced again. Her arms were thin, her shins narrow. She had a pitcher of iced tea and offered to fill plastic cups. She was pleasant and graceful. But to her visible distress, she was received with suspicion. There were those here who would eventually become her friends, who would in the coming years sympathize endlessly on the phone, who would give her advice about growing tomatoes and drying apples and canning elk. But today they were cold to her. They showed her their backs.

Emma said, "I'm getting another Coke. You want one?"

Alma Whittaker, who had promised Buddy's mother she'd look in on him from time to time (she also had an unmarried daughter, and so maintained a proprietary interest in his ranch) limped over to my mother. Said, "Emma tells us you've had your share of struggles. You must be so proud of how you've landed on your feet."

Mother glanced at Emma. "I'm sorry. Struggles?"

Alma managed to look both sympathetic and delighted. "Your marijuana addiction, of course. Your alcoholism! Or maybe you don't like talking about it? But you shouldn't be ashamed! Dear, it's admirable the way you've overcome." She gave the last words the four-note melody of a popular hymn. Alma judged according to her own strengths (temperance, chastity, high fiber) and condemned according to failures she was at no risk to have (promiscuity, whiskey, pornography).

"I'm sorry, what was your name again?"

"Alma, my dear."

"Well, Alma." Mother took in the variety of women, each one pretending interest in another conversation. "My daughter, you should know, didn't want to leave Billings. She's trying to get back at me. I hardly ever drink and I've never smoked marijuana." She sighed heavily, striking precisely the right note: beset mother. "I blame it on puberty, how that girl's taken to lying. It's such a trial."

Design or instinct, it was precisely the right thing to say. She had instantly convened a meeting of mothers against the world. Teenagers! The women around her drew close.

Emma, recognizing a setback, tilted her head to one side. Considered the clouds. A million miles away. She closed her eyes, and smiled as if against a gentle spray of water.

There were things I had already come to love about the ranch. The oil and dirt creviced in my hands, a blue thumbnail coming loose; the scars, bruises, nicks. My sense of apprenticeship. I had already come to know the difference between metric and British, and could find a 5/8 inch wrench in a heartbeat. I had trouble with sharpening knives, and chainsaws, but could see how I might improve. I despised the heat, though; the slow climb of the barn's thermometer to one hundred, then past. And I didn't care for the way Buddy could burden me with his worries. Driving reservoir to reservoir, judging the puddles of damp mud that had once been stock ponds, he'd smack the steering wheel with his palm. "Just look at it. *Look* at it."

My sister enjoyed only the awareness of her own misery. A few nights after the branding, we lay together in bed, stewing. The only time of the day that we were predictably alone. She kicked at the sheets. "That goddamned billy goat. What's his name. Mister all balls and no brains. Beezle. He's got that cow bell and those big nuts and sometimes I can't tell which end's clanging." There was a smell about her, the stale, tidewater fecundity of her period. A month before, I would have quietly agreed to everything. But now, emboldened by new experiences, I said. "You've just got to smack him. Swat him with your hat."

"And how about how dry it is here?" She held up her hand. "I just touch my cuticles and they start to bleed."

"It's the drought. Buddy said it's three years now. Said if we don't get rain soon, all our reservoirs are going to dry up and blow away. We'll have to sell off our cattle."

"Our. Our. Our. We. We. We. Jesus, give it a break, Eli." She dropped back hard into her pillow, kicking at the sheets. "I'm not even tired. I can't believe she makes us go to bed so early."

"She seems happy."

"It never lasts. Her being happy."

"Might this time."

"Anyway, it doesn't matter." She turned to the wall, giving me her back.

"Why's that?"

"I'm taking off. I'm blowing this joint. Hitting the road, Jack. Don't you come around here no more, no more."

"You can't mean that. I mean, Emma." I was instantly panicked. My sister had never issued an empty threat in her life.

"You'll be fine, Eli."

"You're *fourteen*." I heard the wheedle in my own voice. "What will you do for money?"

"I've got plans."

"I'll tell."

"You will *not*." She rolled around quick, snatching at my left forefinger. She twisted it back. "Promise you won't tell."

"Ow, Jesus. Okay, Jesus. I won't tell."

She released my finger. "We have to teach her a lesson, Eli. She just can't pack us up and force us to live out in the middle of nowhere. There are consequences. She has to learn that."

"You're going to teach her a lesson then come back?"

She looked at me pityingly. "That's right, Eli. Yeah, you bet. I'm coming back."

What stood between Pete and Buddy, while serious (involving money), was finally little more than a dispute between children. "I ain't gonna be your friend today," sort of thing. Growing up, they had hunted deer together, fished walleye together, drank beer together. And if it's true that friendship is little more than a shared portfolio of experiences, then they were indeed friends, despite themselves.

But nothing was ever simple or easy with Pete Fahler. He was always one to conflate insult and compliment. He pandered to the crowd by teasing discomfort. Buddy, for instance, had a noble nose, a *schnoz*, heavy on his face. He was aging into it well, but when he'd been twelve, thirteen years old, it had been a burden. Pete Fahler delighted in that insecurity, and had a list of poisonous nicknames. Dumbo, Pinocchio, Buddy Nostrils, and, on at least one occasion, Jimmy Durante. Sitting at our kitchen table, he said now, "Ain't this something. Not enough that Cyrano here had to hire the prettiest woman in Billings, she had to bring the prettiest teenager along with her."

News of the détente between Pete Fahler and Buddy had leaked through Garfield County. At the branding, Pete was seen to shake Buddy's hand, was seen to be contrite. Maybe it was a natural progression for Pete to now be sitting in our kitchen, drinking coffee, eating chocolate chip cookies baked by my sister.

Emma, who had not yet made her first escape attempt, was being disconcertingly subservient. She brought us glasses of milk arranged on a tray. "Prettiest? Yeah right." But she tucked her hair behind her ears, first one then the other, in a way that I knew she felt showed off her cheekbones.

Buddy said, "So who was it left you the heifers?"

"My cousin Bill Taylor. Over around Checkerboard? Me and him always got along real good. Named his little boy after me and all. But, you know. Bad ticker. Put his face right down in his soup." Pete held his arm upright on the table, let it fall.

"I think I met him down at your place one time. Fat, right?"

"Big boned, he always said."

"You must be between a rock and a hard place, coming to me with this deal."

Pete fiddled with his cowboy hat. "It's just that I've always felt bad about how I bought that pasture. Figured I'd make it up to you."

"Another cookie, Pete?"

"Don't mind if I do."

Pete was in possession, it seemed, of 150 first-calf heifers. The calves would need some assistance—a lot of late night babysitting, maybe some chain pulling—but Pete was proposing a fifty-fifty split. His heifers and calves, but we birth them and feed them.

Buddy sat with a yellow legal pad, chewing on a pencil. Finally he said, "I'd like to trust you, Pete. But." He hesitated on the cliff edge of impropriety.

"But what."

"Don't take it a wrong way, but. Everybody knows you're the worst liar in the county."

Like most jovial insulters, Pete himself was impossible to offend. "No way you can call me the worst. Ask anybody if I ain't nothing but the best."

"I guess I need some sort of reassurance, is what I'm saying." Buddy was abashed to be engaging in this sort of conflict. He wouldn't meet Pete's eyes, and mumbled so thickly it was hard to make out the words.

Nevertheless, an hour later, they had reached an accord. We birth the calves, feed the heifers through the winter, and Buddy takes two-thirds of the net from the calf sale. In addition, we could pick out one-third of the heifers to keep as mother cows. Buddy tried to appear nonchalant, but he couldn't stop thrumming his fingers across the arm of his chair. "We can get that in writing, right?"

Sometime later, after Pete had left, Buddy tilted back in his chair, crossed his ankles. "We just took old Pete to the *cleaners*. Know why he was down here begging for pasture? Nobody else wants to go into business with him. That's why. That's what comes of being such a liar. Chickens always come home to roost."

Emma looked off someplace distant. "He seemed nice."

"Oh ho." Buddy considered her. "Let me tell you about nice ..."

A wind gust shook the walls. An empty paint bucket tumbled across the yard. Laundry flapped. "Rain, maybe," Buddy said. Clouds boiled dark, featureless but for an occasional flashbulb flare inside. Barn swallows swooped and darted. "Let's just stand here awhile, watch it come."

But after the first few drops, there was only lightning, thunder. The next morning, we hitched up Buddy's firefighting rig. A flat snowmobile trailer outfitted with a water tank and hand pump. "We get a fire, I want you on top, working that pump." On a ridge above Wolfpen, Buddy was just reaching for his binoculars when I said, "There it is." A thin stream of smoke to the west, the thread of it straight and uncomplicated. It could have been a campfire. He said, "Shit. Okay. Now we go back, we call Pete. Get folks out. We get to it quick, it might not ... shit, okay." He threw his arm across the seat and backed away hard, trailer jackknifing.

Mother drove the truck, idling around the upper edge of the fire. I stood in the back, working the steel-handled pump, blisters blooming across my palms. Buddy walked along with the hose. "Thank God the wind's quiet, that's all I got to say." It was a small fire, polite, but anyone could see how it might suddenly turn vicious. Flames crawled up the tree trunks. Buddy stretched the hose to its furthest reach and sprayed in spirals, stamping, kicking. "Keep pumping goddamnit! What are you stopping for? Keep pumping!" Sweat stung my eyes. I fought tears.

Midmorning Pete arrived with his tractor and disk. He

took in my sweat-stained shirt, the black ash smeared across my forehead. "Heard a rumor there might be a fire around here somewhere." That afternoon, two truckloads of neighbors arrived, half a dozen men swinging out over tailgates. Pete was on his tractor digging fire lines, churning out tractor-wide stripes of sod around the edges of the field. Buddy shoveled dirt over a scattering of fire at his feet. The soil, mulched with pine needles, smoldered and cooked then burst into flame again. Pete said. "Glad Buddy's finally got his chance to lose a few pounds." It was a relief to hear a joke. I passed Pete a water jug. "Firefighters," he said, taking a long steady drink. "Firefightin fools." He treated me like a peer, like an equal. We were men fighting fire. This is my only unequivocally fond memory of Pete. We shared a water jug.

It almost went wrong. The wind picked up toward evening and the flames found new life, skipping in gleeful patches across the grass, jumping firelines, traveling faster than a man could walk. We stood watching, helpless. A blue-bruised bank of clouds rose from the north. The wind felt damp, and smelled of wet concrete. Strands of moisture trailed from the clouds. A pair of squalls blew by on either side. "It's going to miss us." But then drops pattered into the grass, hissing, and then it was raining steadily. Buddy took off his hat, tilting his face to the sky. For the first time all day, he touched me. My back, the top of my head. "You did good."

Yesterday, idling from hardware store to gas station, I saw a camera crew outside Hell Creek bar. I tipped my hat down. KULR 8, doing some man-on-the-street interviews. What can you tell us about Eli Singer? He runs a good ranch, doesn't go to church. Maybe he's been the one sending Curt Fahler cash. He was always a little good for us. A little high and mighty. Brought it back with him from Iraq. Curt Fahler, the other hand, who'd been east only as far as Sioux Falls, west only to Spokane, you can say what you want about Curt but he never put on airs. "Eli Singer ain't the murdering type. His stepdad, though? Old Buddy Singer? That's a whole other story. Odd duck, Buddy."

Down in the courthouse basement, Joanie Sanderford had, perhaps ironically, set up a dry board list of possible suspects. And Phyllis Lundt at the museum had a gambling pool going. Fifty-fifty split that Buddy Singer had done the deed. Three to one it was Pete's ex, Matty. Four to one on me. Payable on conviction, if you read the fine print. She's a sharpie, Phyllis.

That last name, Fahler, is a shortcut around here for self-indulgence and dishonesty. Pete's dad, Charlie, had been a puncher of walls, a threatener of lawsuits. A suicide for whom nobody—not a single soul—grieved. The day of his death, Pete's mother found a note written on the back of an unpaid phone bill. A litany not of regret or sorrow but of vitriolic blame: "You and those goddamned kids." She read the note, then popped a beer and worked up a to-do list (coroner? casket?—how much?—tombstone?). After inspecting Charlie's truck, she'd added, "Replace rear window. Order parts self?"

Curt did his best to live down the family name. A man's ranch is a comment on his character, and Curt's gates have always sagged loose as clotheslines, his fences a rotten zigzag of good-enough. He runs his outfit on baling wire and WD-40. He still plays video games for Chrissakes. Dwayne the UPS driver, he's seen him in there on a Friday morning, cross-legged before the TV, blasting Nazi zombies. Meantime, his yearlings were loose on Hamstetler's BLM, eating grass and shitting spurge.

I'd heard through the grapevine how he'd become obsessed with Buddy, with me. His wife (heavy as an end-loader after the twins), was an unsympathetic ear. "Give it a rest, Curt. Jesus H. Christ. All your blah-blah-blah theories." Curt told his favorite bartender, "Can't sleep, can't work, can't hardly eat. All I got in my head is how I been blaming Dad for running out on us. Makes me feel so goddamned . . ." His voice caught.

Melancholy, he took a Saturday afternoon to pay a visit to the home place. Had been avoiding it for years. Could only imagine the mess. His Dad was always a pack rat. Thirty years now it had been going to the mice and gophers, but maybe there was some old bed frames or something, a curio he could put on eBay.

Thirty years. Curt stood on the weathered-gray porch and ran through a ring of keys, nosing each one into the lock. Finally found one that fit. Twisted it open against gritty resistance. The door had swelled against the jamb, and he had to kick at it with his toe to get it to open. Here it was. All of it. His childhood. A floral-print couch he'd already forgotten about (how many afternoons had he laid there watching TV?) gone blandly gray with dust, one cushion exploded into stuffing. The tracks of mice and pack rats stitching randomly across the floor. A fragile tube of a snakeskin curled around the legs of the stove. Curt smelled mold, wet newspapers, something dead in the subfloor. And beside the light switch, he found a fist-sized flake of empty drywall.

No one had ever approached the house as if it might be a crime scene. It had always simply been the place Pete Fahler had left behind. But right there in the middle of that flaked patch of drywall? Damn if that didn't look like some kind of a bullet hole.

Curt hunkered down, squinted along an imagined trajectory. Across the room on a straight line (say, if you were standing outside, below the porch), the doorjamb beside the kitchen looked cracked, splintered. He walked over to it, set the tip of his finger flat into a dime-sized hole. On the other side of the wall, no exit.

Here in the decrepit house of his childhood he needed a win. His mother, who hadn't had a drink in two years (maybe this time it would take), had married a math teacher in Glendive. A wilted, acne-scarred mushroom of a man, Bill Dietz. A cynic who'd made it his job in life to point out every little flaw in Curt's character. And Curt's wife? Her greatest pleasure lately was to blame Curt for every little thing. The transmission went out on her wagon? Curt's fault. They couldn't afford HBO? Curt's fault. Boobs sagging to her belt? Curt's the one got her pregnant. Curt was heard to tell the bartender, "I called Grady up, told him we might have some of that forensic evidence. And yeah, damn if he don't dig a slug out of that wall. It had fragmented some, but he said he could still send it to the crime lab in DC." Curt savored those words. *Crime lab. Forensic evidence.* "Soon as we get the results back, Grady's saying we can get a search warrant."

Which lit some kind of fuse in Jordan. Second only to divorce or adultery, those are a couple of words that can set the phone lines buzzing. *Search warrant.*

———

Early on a Saturday morning, Grady Fisk and his deputy knocked on my door. I came out with my first cup of coffee to find Grady holding a folded piece of blue paper, saluting, touching the corner of it to his temple. "Sorry about this, Eli." The deputy, Jack Wallach, old enough to be Grady's father, had the heavy face and vicious underbite of a bulldog. Grady said, "We got to search your premises here."

Still in my robe, I let them into my house, sat in the kitchen swirling coffee grounds while Grady and Jack went through my closets. I called in, "You tell me what you're looking for, I might save you some time."

There were protocols in place. A cop etiquette. But Grady figured, hell, it's just Eli Singer. He stood in the bedroom door. "You wouldn't keep a .44 of any sort would you?"

"There's a .38 under the mattress there. You're welcome to it."

Grady found the pistol. Span the cylinder, glanced through the gate at the ammunition. Put it back where he found it. "Probably won't need to."

I brought them a couple mugs of coffee. "I'll be out in my shop, you need me."

"Actually, Eli," Grady ran a flashlight around under the bed. Boxers, and a *Field and Stream* from 1982. "What we need, we need you to stay close."

"I got work to do, Grady."

"Can't have you running around, hiding evidence."

"You think I'd do that?"

"I got people to answer to, Eli."

With the calves shipped and mother cows back in fall

pasture, it was a slow time. The urgency was gone. I had a leisurely kind of day ahead. Just puttering. Fixing what was broke and tightening what was loose. Some ways, it was my favorite part of the year. After you shipped but before you started to calve. I'd been looking forward to it. But now I could only stand there, diminished, sucker-punched by bureaucratic authority. Think you live in a free country? Try not paying your taxes, or running a red light, or having a dead guy erode out of a hillside on your property. "Well, hell."

"Sorry."

"Well. Don't apologize. I get it."

"Appreciate it."

It was all real neighborly. Friends, even still. For a couple more hours anyway. Later in the morning, Grady and Jack headed out to the Quonset. "Hell, you going to search the whole ranch?"

"Just the buildings."

They'd let me back in my bedroom, so I was dressed. "You mind if I tag along?" I use the Quonset as a welding shop and parking, but then there's the storage shelves. Past the chain hoist and the greasy pile of old sawdust, under a fluorescent bulb, I got some rough-milled two-by-sixes pounded together, stacked up with old cardboard boxes. Mother's clothes, Buddy's old puzzles, a few of his books. Worthless mementoes I can't bear to set out at a yard sale.

"You can watch, Eli. I don't mind. Just stand back."

They went for the shelves first thing.

Reassessing them, my eye caught on one of Buddy's old shoeboxes. "Ah shit. Grady?"

He turned back. "What?"

"That shoebox up there."

Grady stretched up to pull it down. Waved at the dust. Tilted the lid up to reveal a wad of greasy chamois. He eyed me from across the Quonset, and there was not the least friendliness in his look. "What caliber?"

"Forty-four, if I remember it right."

"Shit, Eli."

"It was Buddy's. I put it up there after he died. Forgot all about it."

"You *forgot*?" Grady took it more personal than he perhaps should have. "That don't sound real honest there."

I said some words in return. And Jack Wallach (who nobody had ever pegged as a peacemaker) finally had to get between us.

This is when things started to go real bad.

"Yeah," she'd said more than once. "I know the guy." Sewing circles had nothing on New York publishing for gossip. An obscure poet in Montana, sure, but throw in a murder investigation and the headlines wrote themselves. PROOF UNDER A ROCK (*Village Voice*). MURDERER OR MODERNIST (*Slate*). No Rhyme Or Reason (*Daily Beast*). Her colleagues kept pestering her. "So what's the *story?*"

"Just the media making noise." She saw no advantage in saying more. In retrospect, it was his reticence that bothered her the most. You wouldn't call it self-possession. Rather, it was withdrawal, an essential kind of selfishness. Singer had found advantage in taking a step back from the world, letting everyone else come to him. She resented it. What poet didn't like to talk about his own work? Leslie buzzed her into his office, spinning a manila folder across his desk. "Singer's Bookscan numbers. Take a guess?"

"You know I don't like to guess." She ran her finger down the spreadsheet. Widened her eyes for Leslie's benefit. "That's . . . interesting."

"Spread the word. All it takes is a dead body."

Their offices were being redecorated. Between the clank of boards, the whine of drills, the smell of singed carpet, clouds of drywall dust, Montana felt very distant. Leslie said, "Are you still in touch?"

"No."

A single word, but his antennae picked up the vibrations. "Oh sweetie." He put on a face of exaggerated sympathy. "You just need to get back in the saddle. There's bound to be at least one cowboy in New York that writes poetry. And is hung like a bear."

She snorted a chuckle that threatened a sob.

"Really, you okay?"

She took a calming breath, something from yoga. "Is that the time? I got a conference call in like ten seconds."

She went home to her damp apartment in Queens. A heavy porcelain sink and turquoise cabinets with cheap-deal doors that never quite closed, an intermittent line of baby cockroaches fleeing along the grout. She kept threatening a move to Brooklyn, but, well, the rents. Her good days, Queens was still an adventure, an experiment in self-denial. She was a heroine, paying her dues. Her bad days, she was single and broke, shipwrecked in fucking *Astoria*.

She didn't mind growing older. Indeed, there were aspects of it that she quite enjoyed. Being able to pronounce, for instance. But the downside? A dwindling portfolio of viable options. When you're younger, picking through college classes, the decisions feel small, flippant. Should I take Spanish? Whatever. But read the fine print. Every choice you make eliminates two more. Finally, through the slow accretion of days, you're left with only a handful of possibilities, chestnuts you guard like a child counting her nickels.

No, she wasn't still in touch. But what she didn't say? She was in the midst of her own small . . . what was the word? What exactly was she doing here? An inquiry? Yeah, call it that. A polite inquiry. On her good days, she was indulging her curiosity. Her bad days? She was going all *Fatal Attraction* on the guy. It wasn't like she was obsessed or anything. It's just . . . she had questions.

You shop private investigators in Billings, do a web search, the options were limited. A couple corporate outfits, the equivalent of Walmart and Costco, and one independent local. Google street view (friend to pederasts, larcenists, and rejected girlfriends everywhere) showed a nondescript tract office, a mini-mall storefront wedged between a Thai restaurant and a Radio Shack. Her first email, oh-so-carefully composed, was going for insouciance, ennui. She's a literary agent researching a potential project. "Before approaching the potential client with an offer, I'm curious as to liability issues. Culpability. Also, does he have a reputation for reliability? What are the chances he was aware of the crime after it was committed?"

The investigator, a guy named Jackson Ward, called her back within the hour. "Singer, huh. Yeah, I been watching this one." A smooth baritone of a voice, roughened around the edges by smoking. "Making a big splash around Billings these days. Papers love it." She'd never done this before. Did they call themselves Pee Eyes? Private dicks? Gumshoes. She pictured a Marlow-style fedora, tilted low. "As I said, I'm curious about his probable culpability. His background viz the victim. Anything else that might come up."

"So, professional or personal?"

"Excuse me?"

"Your interest, is it professional or personal?"

"I've met him. But it's mostly professional." She braced

herself for further questions. Sure, of course he'd be curious about clients, have to screen them a bit. Can't have crazies just stalking some poor man.

He said, "Hundred-and-fifty an hour, plus travel, meals, motels if I have to go to Jordan. I usually encourage clients to set a limit. How much are you expecting to spend?"

"A discretionary budget gives me about two thousand dollars."

"Fifteen hours. The means I'll be limited to office work. Phone calls, web research. A trip to the library for old newspapers. If you need me to go to Jordan, it'll be at least twice that."

"Start with office work and phone calls, then let's touch base. See where it goes."

"I can start next week."

That had been two weeks ago. She hadn't yet heard back. Was resisting the urge to pester. Some part of her, without entirely being certain of the reasoning behind it, wanted a low profile. A murder investigation on the table, after all. If she found something out, would she then be culpable? Required by law to report it? Maybe. Yeah, maybe. Should she let sleeping dogs lie? She couldn't, she couldn't.

Coming home, Leslie's comment about well-hung cowboys still trailing after her like toilet paper on a heel, she dropped her umbrella in its stand by the door, lifted a housecat—an overweight Manx—off her answering machine (cat-sitting for a neighbor—she'd always been a soft touch) and pressed a button, pulled the cat onto her lap. Kicked off her shoes. After the digital beep, here was the nasal, slightly drunk voice of her mother. "Call me, please. Sweetheart."

Christ. Four words and the woman could just somehow pack in acres of guilt.

The second message? The private investigator. Had she given him her landline? It was unlisted. Maybe he was showing off a bit. "Miss Barnes, this is Jack Ward. Give me a call. I found out some things. And I'd like to discuss your own interest in this matter. Give me a call. Thanks."

Digesting the message, a third call beeped onto the speaker. A long breath, then crackling silence. Chloe expected it to be Helen, who'd been oddly distant lately, who was decidedly *not* returning Chloe's calls. But no. "Chloe." It was a masculine voice. "Hey, it's me." *Singer.* Sonofabitch and speak of the devil. "I'm in, uh, New York. Yeah. Had to get out of Dodge for a while. Anyway, yeah, should have given you a heads-up rather than just springing it on you like this, but we didn't, you know, part on the best . . . ah, shit. I hate these goddamned machines. Give me a call. I got a cell phone now . . ." He gave her the number.

It was raining again. Handfuls of moisture splashing against her window, rattling a loose pane.

What did she do here? Where was the instruction manual? No denying the uncertain little thrill she felt upon hearing his voice. Nor the poisonous little snowball refusing to melt in her stomach now. What was it—uncertainty? A condition that progressively defined her. The new and unimproved Chloe. She squeezed the cat until it squawled and squirmed away. Okay, right or wrong, the biggest mistake was inertia. Who said that? Not her. Absolutely not fucking her.

Did she first call the dick or the *dick*. The man who'd

treated her so shabbily, or the man she'd hired to snoop around on the first man. One or the other, Chloe. Do it now.

She picked up the phone.

"You're smoking now?" This was something of a relief. He had a flaw she could hang her hat on. I mean, in addition to the murder thing.

She hated cigarettes. *Hated* them. Her mother had picked up the habit again after Dad's death. Cigarette smoke, for Chloe, was the smell of grief and uncertainty, self-recrimination, the urge to retreat, to tuck herself away from the world.

She'd met him on the street in front of a favored Pakistani diner. A fusion of Middle Eastern kitsch (bead curtains and Christmas lights, sitars from a 1980s boom box) and American greasy spoon. One of those places where you could get hash browns with your naan.

"You pinch up a chew in New York, folks look at you odd." He stubbed the cigarette out with his toe. "But I'm about done with it. I hate that smell, more than anything."

"Should we grab a table?"

Inside the door, and for Singer's benefit, she hauled out her tiny little bit of Urdu. Said to the cadaverous waiter with too many teeth, "Assalamu alaikum." Was rewarded with a startled, wide grin. He bowed slightly, then uncorked a string of incomprehensible vowels. He waited, eyebrows raised. She pointed to a booth. "We'll take the one by the window."

Something about Singer invited mothering. He had a new and incongruous rumpled air about him. Apology was a gas rising off his skin. They sat down, watched their water glasses get filled. She said, "I should be pissed at you. Oddly, I'm not."

He squinted at the menu, then pushed it aside. "I'm thinking you should probably order for us both."

"What brings you back to the city?"

"Short answer or long? Honest or evasive?"

"Let's go for short and honest."

"You."

"Long and evasive?"

"None of my neighbors'll talk to me. Plus I got a good case of writer's block. That's never happened before. Angst and anomie. Midlife crisis. Also, I keep hearing your voice in my head." He took a sip of water. "You know how there's a difference between criminal suits and civil suits, right?"

"Sure."

"Well, I'm looking at a civil suit. Not yet, but any minute. They found a pistol in Buddy's things. They did the ballistics, and they're saying it's the murder weapon. So now Curt Fahler's running around telling everybody how he's coming after my ranch."

"Jesus. Eli."

"I needed a friend. Guess I had to go all the way to New York."

Don't be touched, Chloe. Don't be moved. Shake it off, shake it off. "Where are you staying?"

"This hostel up on Hundred-and-Tenth? Fifty bucks a night. It's not bad."

"A hostel? You should have said something, Singer. We could have found you a sublet."

"A sublet."

"You should have called, Eli. I kept expecting you to call."

"I know. Yeah. I'm sorry."

As apologies go, it left something to be desired. A few yards less than sincere. Nevertheless, call it a start. She reached across, found his hand. Squeezed the knuckles together. "We'll find you a place."

For the two weeks that Singer was in New York, Chloe dodged the investigator. Two more phone calls, half a dozen emails. She finally wrote, "Thanks for your patience. Busy at the moment. Call when things settle down." What was this? She knew her therapy lingo, had read her share of self-help. This *avoidance behavior*. But why? Was she so desperate for Singer to be something other than what she, at heart, believed him to be? Or was she fearful that she herself might be something other than she had believed herself to be, something that had gone unrecognized. It was the same kind of reluctance—precisely the same, in fact—that kept her away from the bathroom scale certain mornings. *I don't want to know.*

It took Singer three days to move from the hostel into Chloe's apartment. Another two days before he replaced his cowboy hat with a gray wool driving cap. "You don't see people staring?" A day or two after that? He began meeting her eyes.

Chloe's professional métier was narrative. The functioning of story. She had a nose for clunkers, rotated like a spotlight when reading something the least bit original. She was sensitive to certain tropes, certain twists of emotion. She was also a sucker, in her time off, for an old-fashioned romance. She was simultaneously suspicious of, and vulnerable to, the idea that she might be exceptional, that there was a guy out there who might be sharp enough, perceptive enough, to see her for what she truly was. To unlock her secrets. To, to . . . well, okay, Jesus, to rescue her.

I mean, *please*. And yet.

Turning him loose in her apartment, Chloe followed him room to room. Her own critical observer stood off her shoulder, whispering disparagements. Are you so insecure? But she was curious what he might find interesting. She was also— might as well admit it—flattered by his avidity. Coming through her door, kicking off his boots, he was all eyes. "So this is your place, huh? I always wondered."

He went, of course, to her books. Straightaway found her collection of Gorey covers. "Gorey on Kafka?" Breezed past her DVDs (she was ready to apologize for Mickey Rourke), and lingered at her wall of photos. "This your dad?"

"Ages ago."

Chloe and her father at the riding arena, seven-year-old Chloe in helmet and holding a crop.

"He died young, you said."

"This wall over here is my travel wall. One photo for each of my trips."

"Now that's a boatload of photos." Chloe with the Maasai, Chloe on the Charles Bridge in Prague. Chloe with the Terracotta Army.

"I like being a moving target."

It was one of her toss-off lines, but he took it seriously.

"Who's aiming at you?"

"Just an expression, Singer."

"You're alone in all these shots. Who took the photos?"

"Other tourists, mostly."

"You went to all these places by yourself?"

"Sure."

"You got balls, I'll say that."

"Either that or stay home, and I'm not much good at staying home."

"Oh, Chloe." He briefly touched her shoulder.

Was that pity? It was, it was. And where the fuck did *that* come from?

To write a decent poem, she'd read (was it Berryman?) you have to be a prick. Bukowski, Eliot, even Frost. Assholes, all. There were exceptions, sure (Mary Oliver, Wendell Berry) but seems like most decent poets are objectionably self-absorbed. Singer, she'd thought, was the anomaly. A poet with a generous soul. But now she found herself wavering. He lately seemed curious only about himself. Standing at a Times Square crosswalk, waiting for the light, considering the pedestrians, he said, "We're all trying so goddamned hard to feel good about ourselves."

"Speak for yourself, Singer."

Later that night, having a nightcap at her kitchen table (he preferred his wine in a water glass), he said, "My whole life, the worst thing that could happen is I'd have to sell my ranch. Even if I couldn't pay my credit cards, I'd still think, well, at least I got my ranch. But now. Shit."

"You should write some poems about New York."

He snorted. "Yeah right."

"Seriously. You want to get used to not having a ranch? Write about something else."

"Easy thing to say."

That weekend, they took a train into the city. He'd never been to the Met, and wanted to see the Rembrandt room. An hour into it, they were stumbling gallery to gallery, glutted with beauty. And then he snagged on Carpeaux.

"Singer?" She came back to him.

He was struck dumb, staring up at *Ugolino and his Children*. After a time, he took off his cap. Cleared his throat. Blotted his eyes with a shirt cuff.

She waited. "Grab a drink upstairs?"

They had their wine, and he said, "That one just kicked the shit out of me. Those kids. Whew. Those expressions."

"You were twelve, you said." It was a risk to even bring it up.

"When Pete disappeared. Yeah."

"So you didn't know about it? The murder?"

He polished off his wine.

"Singer?"

"No, I didn't know about it."

Even still, even now, she wanted to believe him. She truly did.

The day before his flight back to Montana, she met him by the elevators. Gave him a quick half hug. "Right on time."

Singer noted the drywaller's buckets in the halls. "You're remodeling?"

"They're almost done. Thank god."

Leslie stood to meet them. "Eli! You're looking well. Chloe, lovely as ever."

She said, "Love your suspenders." Lavender, over a pink shirt. "Not many guys could pull that off."

"Eli, coffee?"

With the remodel, and reflective of recent deals, Leslie's new office was half again larger than his old one. A view of the Hudson and, on his shelves, half a dozen bestsellers. A thriller series. A cookbook or two.

Leslie tilted back in his chair, folded his hands over his belly. "So," he said. "Memoir."

Singer blinked. "Sorry?"

"I want a memoir."

"Well. I write poetry."

"Poets can write whatever they want. I've seen it time and again. A novelist writes poetry? It's shit. A poet writes a novel? He pulls it off. You're more versatile than you think."

"So you want me to write about . . . what exactly?"

"The poet considers his own murder investigation. Love it. Love it. We could make so much money."

Singer glanced at Chloe. *Did you know about this?*

She gave him nothing. *You're not the only one who can be opaque.*

He cleared his throat. "How much?"

"We'll set a floor of two hundred grand, then hold one hell of an auction."

"Two hundred thousand dollars."

"Or more, yes." This was Leslie's preferred domain. Talking money. "But we'd want to offer a big reveal. Could you do that? Give the readers some fresh news?"

Singer reached toward his hip pocket for his Skoal. Reconsidered. Instead, he tapped his fingers on the arm of his chair. "Let me think about it."

The Brook Trout

At nine thousand feet,
A brook trout wrapped in foil
sizzled in orange coals,
its viscera stripped away,
replaced with butter, salt,
pepper. The foil still hot enough
to burn, my fingers plucked pieces
of white flesh from translucent bones.
I sipped at the meat, swallowed bits
and pieces of this exquisite
little life.

If god exists, to judge by the world
he saw fit to create, he must be little more
than teeth and a tongue. If you ask me,
god is one famished
sonofabitch.

I'm SLIGHTLY DEAF IN my left ear, courtesy of an IED in Iraq. Not many people know about this. Blood from a scalp abrasion dripped into my eyes and a symphony of bells faded to a high-pitched whine. A bus lay smoking on its side, gray undercarriage exposed. Memory skips a groove. Then I'm reaching into the rubble for the hand of a child. Her burned skin threatened to peel off like a glove. You do not talk about it because there is nothing to say. You can't change it, you can't accept it. Love and hate are the persistent irreducibles of our species.

Buddy was a student of family trees and alleles, the generational square dance of dominants and recessives. Cattle and horse breeders, they all think alike. The calculated, artful topping of the right bull over a likely cow predetermines the worth of the calf. Why would it be otherwise for people? Freedom is a lie we tell ourselves to avoid the notion that we are all on the way to becoming our parents.

As Buddy became more clearly interested in my mother, he would ask me for details of other members of our family. Out of politeness, he'd start the conversation with a revelation of his own. "My old dad, as he got older, he'd have to get up about five times a night just to take a leak. So I got *that* to look forward to." He'd clear his throat. "So'd *your* dad have prostate problems then?"

He shouldn't have bothered with subtlety. What little I knew I passed along without hesitation. "Mom and Dad both came from Butte." Dad's family had been miners, Catholics, whiskey drinkers, life-lovers. But Mom's people were . . . unstable. "Aunt Mabel? She collected insects." Beetles and butterflies pinned on boards. Healthy enough work, perhaps, but after several years at it she began seeing bugs everywhere, particularly on her own skin. The day they committed her to the state hospital at Warm Springs she was a carpet of moon-shaped scabs. "Grandma killed herself." She swallowed pills. Three bottles of aspirin to eat slow holes in her stomach. A cousin who dressed in women's clothes, a great aunt who prostituted herself for morphine. And our grandfather, who, after the death of his wife, disappeared on the grub line: brimstone tea and pies stolen off windowsills. He jumped a train in snowy November with a promise to be back by March (but having failed to mention the year). "When Mom married Dad, she was seventeen. They moved to Billings." My mother's last memory of Butte was of her brother standing at a drum in the alley, burning family photos. Lighter fluid and a spiraling haze of sparks, a tiny gray tornado of ashes.

"Mom," I added reluctantly, "she gets headaches." This was a poor word for what happened. The pain that forced her to lie in the dark with a damp rag over her eyes. She claimed it turned a blue sky red, that it seared electric haloes around the heads of her children. "It's like I got a toy train behind my eyes," she said. "A tiny little diesel engine chugging around in circles. Or maybe it's a lighthouse. Yeah, that's it. How it swings around. You catch your breath and then *whoosh* here it comes again."

"And Emma? Is she more like your mom or your dad?" He'd dismissed it too lightly, the notion of Mother's headaches. But I'd done my part.

"Emma's just, you know, *Emma*." I put some scorn into my voice.

The scorn was a betrayal. My very first one.

Her first attempt at escape, my sister got as far as Jordan. Fifty miles of gravel and gumbo, but she somehow made it. Hitched a ride, I suppose, perhaps from some Fort Peck fishermen. In any case, our county sheriff, who was then Burt Phillips, drove past her on his way into work. Saw her out on Highway 52 with a blue backpack between her feet and one leg out in the breeze, thumb cocked. A cliché from *Easy Rider*, a seductress stopping traffic. Two hours later he pulled into our yard, Emma in the back seat.

Burt was a large man, fat enough to keep moving for a second after he finished walking. His wife had let out his uniform with bolts of paler khaki sewed into the seams. She wasn't much of a seamstress, and loose threads dangled from him like tassels. He shook Buddy's hand, breathing wetly after the effort of walking from his car. "That little girl there is in need of some manners."

"Oh?"

"That mouth of hers? Good lord."

"Well."

Burt held out his arm. "Look there. She went and offered to bite me." The fabric held a matching pair of moist, half-circle indentations. "Mother and me with our brood, we always got good results from a whipping. The Bible says don't spare the rod and I think that's about right. Especially when it comes to girl children." Burt opened the back door for Emma.

I stood at the screen door, finishing off my toast. Mother went past me in carpet slippers.

Despite the day's coming heat, Emma wore her denim jacket, the one with a pattern of red and yellow rhinestones across the shoulders. It was the finest thing she owned. She'd clearly hoped to make an occasion out of her own running away. Through the screen, I met her eyes. Caught a glimpse of uncertainty but then watched it instantly evaporate. She said, "Came *this* close to making it."

Mother reached out for Emma's bicep. Hard enough, surely, to leave a bruise. "Get your little ass in the house. I have never in my life, never been more . . . Honestly! *Emma*."

Emma had at some point become as tall as Mother, albeit slimmer. Pulling away, she drew Mother half a step toward her. She worked at Mother's fingers. "You're *hurting* . . . no, see. No! You're why . . . *Fuck you*!" With her free hand, trying to release herself, she pushed at Mother.

Mother instinctively pushed back.

They stood there, swaying like trees, shoving, concentrating. Me and Buddy and Burt, watching. Do we intervene?

They fell together into the dust, face to face, squirming.

Squinting at them, was this anger or affection? From a distance it might have been both. Mother finally freed one arm and slapped Emma on the cheek. Hard. They both lay quiet after that, panting. You could see the shape of Mother's hand rising on Emma's face.

Burt looked on with satisfaction. Said to no one in particular, "See?"

There were things my mother wanted from the future. Primarily, I believe, she wanted us all to stay together, to stay close. "I cannot wait until you're old enough to give me a grandchild, Emma. I'll hold that sweet baby on my lap and tell her all the ways you used to torment me." That Emma might run away, I think—might have *succeeded* at it—must have frightened Mother badly. Out of fear, then, she reacted badly.

That night, Emma lay on our bed fully dressed. A sneaker had slipped off onto the floor. Athletic sock going thin at the toe. She whispered to herself, counting on her fingers. After a time she turned to me. "Okay. Here's what you do. You'll just tell them you fell asleep. When you woke up? I was gone."

"Okay."

"Say it just like that. I woke up, she was gone."

"*Okay.* Jesus."

Two in the morning, I awoke to the sound of our station wagon starting up. The cough of missing cylinders, bald tires spinning out of the driveway. A few minutes later, Buddy loomed over my bed. "I woke up," I yawned. "She was gone."

He only stared at me.

Her big mistake lay in not paying attention to the gas gauge. If she'd refilled from one of the ranch tanks before leaving, she might have outpaced him. As it was, when she pulled into the only gas station in Jordan (she was an inexperienced driver, a staller and a lurcher and a gear-grinder), he was right behind her, flashing his brights.

Driving back to the ranch, she would have been sullen in the dim light of his dashboard, resentful, chewing at her hangnails. Buddy would have parsed out his few words slowly, carefully. He made certain concessions, asked for certain things in return. "I'll start paying you a salary. How's that. I'll help you open a bank account. We'll hire you out cleaning houses. Would you like that?" His manner would have been enough to dampen the sputtering fuse of her disdain. Like all teenagers, she wanted nothing more than to be treated as an equal. Buddy could have given her that.

Emma and my mother inhabited their own subtle world of accusation and score-keeping. It was a mystery to Buddy. I remember that Mom once picked an argument over Buddy's refusal to donate his mother's clothes. "I'm still living out of a suitcase, Buddy. And you've got closets *filled* with old dresses." She had also confronted him over his household grocery budget. ("There's four of us here now, Buddy. *Four*. You've got to spend *some*thing.") But this was nothing to what happened when Mother found out that he was making promises to Emma, that he was interceding on the girl's behalf. "She's *my* daughter. *Mine*. Not yours." In place of punctuation, Mother slammed doors. She was still an employee, however, and so came back, simultaneously outraged and contrite. "I'm sorry, Buddy. But, I mean. *Really*."

"Okay, Bess. Okay." He retreated.

But he was obligated now, and Emma not only began receiving a salary from Buddy, she began cleaning houses as well. She was released, despite my mother's best efforts, upon the world.

———

I believe this was also the fall when I got bronchitis. A fever, a dry cough. It brought me inside for a week or so. Out on the ranch with Buddy, I had imagined that Mother was isolated and alone, lonely, staring through windows, scrubbing floors, peeling carrots. Mumbling to herself, stewing. But listening to her gossip now into the phone—"So how'd she find out? . . . Henry *Miller*? You can't get that at the *library* . . . If he's so smart, why didn't he notice her best pair of underwear was missing?"—my worry diluted to self-pity. *She* was the happy one.

I dug through Buddy's things. Jazz albums shelved under his old Victrola, books that I opened with the cold, dusty smell of tombs, a lifetime's worth of old cowboy boots piled in his closet. At the top of his closet, a shoebox with a pistol. A worn leather holster folded like a snake and a paper box of shells. I didn't touch it.

Of more interest to me, in the back of his underwear drawer, under a 1964 *Playboy*, I found his photo album. Why would he hide this away? The first pages filled with newspaper clippings and faded stock show ribbons. After that, photos and marginalia. Beside an ancient eight-by-ten of a woman posed in a wedding dress, Buddy had written, "Great Aunt Julia Sweeney. Diphtheria, 1922." A five- or six-month-old baby lay in a tiny coffin, trimmed in lace. "Great Uncle Charlie. Croup, 1910." As the photos grew more recent, the descriptions expanded into histories. About his father (dour and stern, a walrus mustache hiding his lips), he wrote, "Never knew a happier man. He said he didn't worry about tomorrow since it hadn't come yet, said he never fretted about yesterday because it was already gone." By the time I came to Buddy's mother (ten full pages), the margins were entirely covered by scribbling. A faded color snapshot of the old woman holding a fistful of flowers, glaring at the cover. "Don't forget how Momma liked sweet clover." Holding a pie with a blue ribbon taped to the pan. "Ten ribbons in a row before she stopped entering, saying it was time to give somebody else a chance." Finally, a single photo of his sister, a young woman on a sorrel quarter horse. Her face had been torn across, scribbled white in anger, then (in a later regret) half-repaired, the flaps smoothed and taped back into place. The margins were blank. After this, there was only one other photo. A small Polaroid of Emma. When had he taken it? She was sitting on Pepper, wearing a white cowboy hat tilted back. He had just begun to write in the margins: "She wants to be a fashion designer. She wants to go to Paris. She wants me to build her a swimming pool." This was all news to me.

Mother sang in the kitchen. I heard the clang of a stove lid, the flaring hiss of a match. "I am just a poor boy though my story's seldom told . . ." Outside, an Angus bull had found its way into the yard. Facing him across the fence, a second bull stood braced, bellering. They had been fighting through the barbed wire, pushing face to face. Blood from fence cuts mingled with the slobber, forming crimson ropes of foam.

I felt very alone.

This was a period of my childhood when I was narrating my own life. *This is as happy as I've ever been*, I would think, sitting down to one of Buddy's Sunday breakfasts, to platters of eggs and thick slabs of pink ham.

I watched Buddy and my mother wear grooves into each other. He began eating her meals with mechanical distraction, equally as blind to poached walleye as to peanut butter and jelly. "Good grub there, Bess. Thanks." Evenings, they sat with wineglasses or beer, an account book open between them. "I could sell off a little hay, roll the dice on an easy winter."

She cleared her throat. "Don't let me forget, Mattie Bell wants us down for supper Friday."

"Couple of them new heifers got scours. Thinking about getting Pete to pay for a vet visit."

He took to bringing her mementoes from his day. I'm sure he saw this as a wooing. The fragment of an arrowhead. A pair of deer skulls locked together at the antlers. A knot of barbed wire melted into a brittle blob of slag. "Here you go, Bess." He'd stand with the awkward anxiety of a boy giving flowers. To my mother's credit, she would accept these worthless artifacts graciously, kissing his cheek. The kiss had become expected, accounting at least in part for the forest of debris that soon littered our kitchen.

For her part, my mother did her best to make him comfortable. He was chary with advice, however—"Hell, it don't matter to me. I'm easy"— and so she learned to study him illicitly, from the corner of her eye. He preferred beef to chicken, cotton socks over wool, and idleness in the evenings made him nervous. She was teaching herself to knit and had started on a cardigan in garish reds and greens, feet planted wide, socks loose on her speckle-haired calves. She knew how to straddle barbed-wire fences, how to brush chicken heads away from the block with the flat of her hatchet. Frumpy, wind-burned, she'd gone stolid as a fireplug.

Evenings, they danced. I had mentioned his jazz records—"Where'd you get these?"—and with only just that much encouragement he'd slid out one of his favorites. "These jazz people," he said, "they got their own words for things. My sister, she'd say, 'Listen to the chops on that guy.' Or . . ." He rubbed at his eyes, ambushed by the thought of his sister.

"Who's this?"

"Oh, this is that old Duke Ellington. There was a time he was about the only guy we could get on records."

He turned the volume up high. It was a music that invaded rooms. Mother tapped the time on her knee, watching Buddy hover over the player. Impatiently, she finally stood and held out her hand. "Well sure, I'd be happy to dance."

Emma and I watched as they swung each other back and forth, Mother in his arms then not, he grasping her waist then not, an unseen wad of proscription at their groins. Unexpectedly, Emma liked the music. "It's so square and awful it's just cool." Buddy bowed and took her hand. "Secret to jitterbugging is to pick a man that knows what he's doing." He spun her around, brought her chest thumping to his chest, threw her away again. "Secret for a woman's just being loose, letting come what may."

I sat on the edge of the room, watching their forms pass back and forth. How would this room have seemed from the outside? The lamps throwing their light across the lawn, and the shadows passing between. For a set of eyes staring in from the darkness—a coyote, maybe, pausing on his hunt—the house would have seemed not a shelter but a confinement. The walls of Bedlam, barricaded against the dangerous and incontinent creatures within.

———

His lighter flared bright in the dark cab. Mother had been badgering him away from snoose—"Can you imagine kissing a mouth filled up with that junk?"—and so he'd begun smoking. Inexperienced, he clinched the cigarette tight in his teeth, puffing it like a cigar. "You haven't been to Jordan before, have you?"

"We drove through on our way in."

"Ugly little town, ain't it."

"I guess."

He stubbed out his cigarette. "My old dad one time, he went into town and they was doing some roadwork. Digging up a water main, putting in a sewer pipe, whatever. He went up and asked what were they doing and they said, whatever, digging up a water main. And he said, 'Damn. I thought you was burying this ugly little town and I was going to help you.'" He shook his head. "*Bury this little town.*"

It was a long drive. He said, "I think I'm going to ask your mother to marry me. What do you think about that?"

"Fine. I guess."

"Do you think she'll say yes?"

"I don't know."

"You think she likes me?"

"Sure." After a time, I said, "Yeah, I think she'll say yes."

Like all sons, I was nothing if not a student of my father's face. I expected him to be pleased, but he wasn't. He wasn't anything. "They killed the last wolf out of this county in 1921. Last buffalo, aught-three. The grizzlies went, then those Lewis and Clark bighorns. Killed the elk out, then trucked in a fresh batch from Yellowstone. And deer? Hell, back when we first come into this country, deer was scarce as hen's teeth. That big rack in the barn? Daddy and me tracked that thing six hours in a fresh snow." He shook another cigarette from the pack. "Then Daddy died, Terry died, Momma died . . ." he tilted his head away from the flash of the lighter. "You said you haven't tasted whiskey before?"

"Uh uh."

"Well, we'll get you one tonight. First time you and me had a whiskey together. Take home a napkin or something."

"All right."

He flicked his ash out the window. "You get used to change being a bad thing. I guess that's my point. My whole life, I don't know I ever had something change that I didn't want to see it change back. You see what I'm getting at?"

"Not really, I guess."

"Your mother says yes, it'll take some getting used to."

We hesitated in the open door, pausing at the edge. The saloon was a cavern of smoke and dusty lights, a backbar mirror and a pulsing jukebox. Clocked rituals of drinks raised and lowered; friends beside you and enemies across from you and a cement floor washed out once a week with a hose. "Guess we might as well get to it." Buddy pushed me ahead of him. The door clattered shut behind us. "There's the party." At the back, an old man danced alone beside a stack of birthday presents, an open Pabst in his hand. Buddy had said, "Donald used to be one hell of a horse trainer. Skidded logs, too." Eighty-three years old today, he managed now only a slow shuffling jig, a crimped coordination of bad knees and crooked spine.

Buddy said, amused, "Look how he's already three sheets gone." Someone called Buddy's name, and he lifted a hand. He passed me our present for the old man, a Timex watch wrapped in the Sunday comics. "Take that back on over to the table."

I returned to laughter at the bar. A row of backs. Snoose rings worn white in back pockets. "About time Buddy come in to buy a round. Ol' Buddy, ain't seen you in here since . . . well, shit, how long's it been?" Beer bottles and whiskey glasses and dollar bills scattered between the coasters. "Hey Buddy, you take a look at old Donald there? Ain't he the shits? Last time I saw anybody move like that it was at a funeral."

As the sun set, the bar filled. A coarse-haired dog, a terrier mix, sighed and sank onto a horse blanket. I knelt beside him. He rolled over, offering me his stomach: three legs tucked in and the fourth an amputated, calloused knob. The bartender disappeared into the back and Buddy handed me a shot glass filled with whiskey, a plastic cup of water. "Quick, now." The liquor tasted like soot and cinders and gasoline, and all of it still afire. I clenched my jaw and shook my head. "Whooowheeee!" I disdained the water, strangling, "Don't think I'll be needing that." My back was slapped by a swarm of hands. "Look at old Eli here! Hey, you got a good one here Buddy." The night grew old. I drank another whiskey. The room wanted to tilt. I wasn't drunk until I closed my eyes. Who knew that people could be so friendly? Later in the night, there was an off-tune rendition of "Happy Birthday," and the old man grinned wide, soaking it up.

At some point, Pete and Buddy stood together at the bar. "Think I got us a buyer for our calves. Old boy out of Bozeman."

Buddy tilted back a shot. "Cattle buyers. Bunch of liars all the way up and down. Takes one to know one I guess."

They discussed shipping rates and shrink. Three or four other men joined them. Pete said, "Old Buddy here's been telling me about how he's been trying to tear off a piece off that little housemaid he's got up there. Been wanting some advice."

Buddy glanced at me. "Pete."

"Yessir. Been wondering about how you go about it. I said, hell, son, just do like a dog does with a bitch. He says to me, 'Sniff her ass and run around in circles?'" There was laughter, not at the joke so much as Buddy's reaction, his blush. Pete caught the bartender's eye and circled his finger around their empty glasses. "Yessir them housemaids. I knew it first time I laid eyes on her. Big old handsome cowboy with a ranch, her with two little kids, I said to Matty I said that there's going someplace. Yessir them little housemaids. And that daughter, too? Boys, I'm telling you, you should see her twitching around my house, cleaning it up. Mother to daughter, I'm telling you what."

Emma was cleaning Pete's house? News to me.

Apparently, news to Buddy as well. A few minutes later, he said, "Hey, Pete? Just shut the *hell* up."

A blink, and then he had Pete's shirt twisted in his fists, pushing him against the bar. The bartender said, "Take it outside, take it outside."

Buddy left first, not looking back. A crowd followed. Pete emerged last, drinking straight from a pint of Jim Beam. Buddy stood half-encircled. Some said Pete's name, some said Buddy's. Pete smashed the bottle to the ground. He held up his fists. "C'mon then."

There was no real fight. Pete swung first and Buddy took it on his shoulder. Then Buddy stepped forward, already punching. He gave Pete a single, ham-handed smack across the temple. It wasn't the blow so much as the momentum that drove Pete to the ground. A drunk losing his feet. He lay flat, already unconscious, slack mouth mewed open to the wet dirt.

"There you go." Buddy spat toward him. Though not quite on him. "There you go."

Two weeks into hunting season, Mother wanted to see Buddy's buck. She ran ahead of me through the rain into his shop to stand beside the hanging deer, hand flat on the ribs. "Did it die fast?"

"He put a good shot on it, yeah."

She glanced at the unskinned head on the ground, the lower jaw askew, tongue aloll. "Pete came by. Apologized to Buddy for that scene at the bar."

"Oh?"

"You were at school. They shook hands. Buddy said he never held nothing against any man for being drunk. Men. I mean, *really*. You won't be like that, will you, Eli?"

"Like what?"

"It's not something you have a choice about, I suppose."

Preoccupied, she began picking her way around the shop, running her fingers along a pegboard of screwdrivers, wrenches, chisels. "It's such an odd place." She pulled back a tarp to inspect Buddy's snowmobile. "So far from where we were. You know, I still miss your father sometimes." She reached up to touch an elk antler hanging from a cross beam. "And I miss the funniest little things."

"Like what?"

"He used to talk about where we'd go on our honeymoon. We never had a honeymoon. Did you know that?"

"No."

"Well, we never did. Couple of kids so poor we had to rent a housecat. That was one of his sayings. Said he was going to take me to Bimini. Off the coast of Australia, he said. I think he just liked saying the word. *Bimini*." She touched a stack of rough-sawn lumber. "After he died I went and looked it up. Bimini. And do you know, it's nowhere near Australia." She studied her fingertips for splinters. "Do you think I should marry Buddy? I'm just curious for your opinion."

"What about Pete?"

She pulled away. "Pete?"

"The way you've been around him. Emma's noticed it too."

"She has?"

"Yeah."

"Pete. Well, Pete's a leaky vessel, isn't he? Shoot, he's a sieve. He makes me feel young. And pretty. But I've got a marriage proposal on the table. I've got to think about other things. You and Emma."

"Don't do it for us."

"What about your sister? What would she think?"

"Maybe you should ask her."

"She doesn't want anything to do with me anymore." Mother pried up a board from a stack of lumber, then let it fall in a clanking cloud of dust. "Your sister's always needed a lot of attention."

"Well."

"It's cold out here." She flipped up her collar, shivering. "I'm going back in."

I stayed in the barn long enough for her to make it back into the house. I loved my mother, but there were times when I didn't especially like her. I loaded a few sticks of wood into the stove. I twirled the deer on its chain. The patter of rain on the roof tin dwindled away. When I stepped outside, however, I found her still in the yard, staring up into the clouds. She held out her hand as I approached. "Do you hear them?"

"Hear what?"

"Those geese."

"You're standing out here just listening to the geese?"

"Listen."

"I don't hear anything."

"Headed south." She followed their imagined progress above the clouds. "No stopping them now."

The day of their wedding, a cold rain swept in from the north. Behind the barn, a loose piece of tin flapped and banged. Mother studied the sky and hugged her arms. Pickup trucks pulled into the yard, clogged to the fenders with gumbo. The men wore Sunday suits hidden under ducking jackets and yellow slickers; the women wore heavy wool dresses and rubber overshoes. We sat shivering on damp metal chairs borrowed from the Presbyterian church. Plastic bunting from the fourth of July flapped overhead.

The photographer had erected a white wicker arbor, decorating it with a sprinkling of plastic ivy. Earlier, Buddy and

Mother had stood under this bower, Mother smiling politely, holding a bouquet, Buddy squinting. Later, Norwood Ryerson played the bridal march on his piano accordion. That was my signal. I took Mother's arm at the top of the aisle. She made us walk slow, and kept pulling me back. Buddy waited, jowls swollen above his collar, clearing his throat. The preacher wet a finger and flipped through his Bible, glanced at the sky. "We'll make this one quick." A few moist flakes of snow began spinning down.

Afterward, there was a flat cake iced in pastels, a pair of tilted figurines, a sliced ham. A banjo and a guitar to join Norwood's accordion. Three men played under canvas while Mother and Buddy danced a hesitant jig, an uncertain jitterbug that gradually wound down to a slow simple swaying, hand in hand, waist to waist. They kissed once, and there was applause. Buddy's lips worked hard at keeping back a grin.

Mother had insisted on a keg and a card table of booze. Jack Daniels, Cutty Sark, Lewis and Clark vodka. Rain came in chilled pockets. We stood in a line under the eaves, curtained behind dripping water. Young men pumped at the keg. Buddy took up his fiddle to play with the band, calling each tune with a nod and a word. The music found its stride, scrolling up and down the scale. In its sincerity, its utter lack of irony, its simple impulse toward entertainment, it recalled music from a previous century. Mother danced with most all of the men, kissing them on their cheeks and being kissed in return. She seemed very happy.

Pete Fahler had arrived late, and stood drinking from a private flask. At dusk, men turned their truck headlights onto the yard, circling the muddy dance floor. Pete stood behind this circle of light, avoiding eye contact. Emma said, "Be right back." She walked through from our darkness toward his. Approaching him, he showed his teeth, and offered her his flask. She glanced around quickly, tilted it back. Coughed against her hand. They stood together, half-lit, unspeaking. Pete's hand found her shoulder.

She did not brush it off, she did not squirm away.

Mother had turned in earlier, touching Buddy's sleeve. "All that wine's just making me a little wobbly." She'd lingered, giving him an opportunity. "Buddy?" He was preoccupied. "Right behind you. Honey." He had a lifetime of married nights ahead, and only one of being the groom. All this attention. Maybe he'd been wrong about these people. He stood shaking hands, the truck-lit dance floor gradually unpiecing itself as each vehicle began its slow, muddy churning up the driveway. "Cecil? Glad you could make it. Wendy? Nice to see you again." The men congratulated him. "You'd better get in there, you old dog, get to work being a husband."

Tonight there was nothing wrong with him and maybe there never had been.

He found Mother awake, sitting up in his bed with his pillows folded and stacked behind her. A peach-colored nightgown and lace shoulder straps. Without a bra, under the silk fabric, her breasts hung smooth and low. He stood awkwardly. "Didn't mean to keep you up."

She smiled tiredly, setting aside her book. "Come to bed, Mr. Singer."

He didn't know what to do with his hands. "Well, okay. Okay then, Mrs. Singer." He said it again. "Mrs. Singer."

SHE COULDN'T FACE THE detective. Couldn't do it. Did she have to? No she did not. She FedExed a check. Two grand, with a note. "Thank you for your work." Three days later, a packet arrived. FedExed to her office. A half-inch of manila folder and Xeroxed news articles, web photos, printed mimeos. A jump drive. A letter. An abrupt salutation, a colon. Chloe Barnes: All business.

She stopped right there. Shut the folder. Lifted her index finger and pushed the whole package to one side. How much did she want to know? There are issues here. Culpability, self-awareness, self-interest. If she fell in love with him (if she continued; *continued* to fall in love), was she sabotaging their happiness? But if she chose ignorance, what did that say about the foundations of the relationship? Did she really want to live the rest of her life wondering?

She said to her assistant, "I'm getting this awful headache, Francey. I have my phone. See you tomorrow?" Took the R train to a bar she favored off Houston. "Double greyhound, please." Drank half, then sat considering the folder.

Okay.

Okay, here we go.

Okay, this time, really. Here we go.

Chloe Barnes:

Per your request, we have investigated Eli Singer in the context of his potential culpability in the 1979 murder of Pete Fahler. We conclude that Eli Singer is circumstantially responsible for sending cash gifts to the Fahler family. These gifts began not long after Fahler's disappearance—perhaps initiated by Buddy Singer—and continued until three weeks before Fahler's body was found. There have been no cash gifts since, and there are no other viable candidates for these payments. By implication, Eli Singer was aware of Pete Fahler's murder, making him an accessory. Having said that, without a direct confession, it's unlikely a court would convict him of wrongdoing.

Presenting ourselves as reporters for the *Chicago Tribune*, we conducted phone interviews with three principals: Curt Fahler, son of Pete Fahler; Abraham Zellner, hired man on the Singer ranch; and Felicity Gable, currently a Vice Principal at Roosevelt High School in greater Seattle. Five years ago, Miss Gable worked as a schoolteacher in a one-room schoolhouse not far from the Singer ranch. She maintained an intimate relationship with Eli Singer for a period of eight months. Her interview was especially revealing, as you'll note.

Finally, we were disappointed to learn that your interest in Eli Singer is not as professional as you would have initially led us to believe. Please note that this letter, and the enclosed materials, represent the termination of our agreement.

Sincerely . . .

Yada yada yada.

She ignored the rebuke. Whatever. She opened the folder and looked first at a recent *Billings Gazette* profile of Singer. Headline: POET FINDS INSPIRATION IN TRAGEDY. It was accompanied by a photo. He'd grown a beard. Black, but stained gray at the corners of his mouth. The piece had been written by Heather somebody or other. According to the article, he was teaching himself French. "Seems like every poet should take a shot at translating Apollinaire, one time or another."

She had to find out from the newspapers that he was teaching himself French.

She skipped past interviews with Abe and Curt Fahler, their paper-clipped photos. Went straight to Felicity Gable. Pretty enough. Her photo came from the school district's website. Pale-skinned, dark-eyed. Hair tied back to show clean cheekbones, sensible earrings. A professional, you could tell; reserved. Someone Chloe herself could manage to be friends with, maybe.

She skimmed the interview, and let herself snag on a portion.

Int: So you left Montana after just one year?
FG: I was accepted to a graduate program at Idaho State. School administration?
Int: Did you keep in touch?
FG: Eli broke it off. Said he couldn't imagine traveling back and forth to Idaho. I was okay with it.
Int: You were okay?
FG: Sure, it made sense. I mean, I could never see him leaving that ranch.

Int: Did you guys ever visit after that?

FG: What paper did you say you were with?

Int: Sorry. I'm just trying to get a handle on his personality, who the guy really is. You know?

FG: I didn't visit him. I guess I was a little . . . I don't know. Tired? He could be trying.

Int: In what way?

FG: He was so . . . practical? And that's okay, but it doesn't leave much room for romance. I'd say, let's go to Billings, eat some good food. He'd say, let's just pull some good cuts of steak out of his freezer. Same food, half the price. You see what I'm getting at?

Int: Was he so practical that he could have murdered Pete Fahler.

FG: Murder? Eli? (Laughter.) Seriously?

Int: Why not?

FG: I saw him put down a horse one time. Favorite saddle horse of his. What was that horse's name . . . Patches, maybe? Anyway, I watched him lead the horse into the woods, and he had this pistol. I heard the shot, then he came back out. I've never seen a man cry so much. He couldn't hardly talk. So, yeah. Murder? Nuh uh.

Chloe ordered another greyhound. Considered the folder while she waited. Could be better, could be worse. Accessory, which she'd figured. But tenderhearted. Did it change anything?

They'd fallen back on phone calls. How all this started. Complaint and consolation broken down into a few billion digital ones and zeroes, bounced off a satellite and piped through a phone line. Chloe in her pajama bottoms and Dartmouth T-shirt, baggy socks and portable phone, kicked back in her recliner. The fabric had worn through on the arms. Talking, she would push stuffing back under the threads. "How's that proposal coming?"

"Still thinking about it."

It was in this period that Helen broke her mysterious radio silence. Chloe said, going for lighthearted, hiding hurt feelings, "I thought you must have finally met the one, you know. Run off, got eloped. I was about ready to head to Vegas with a search party."

It was the afternoon of a Thursday, a business day, yet Helen was calling from a bar somewhere. A bar or a café. Background sounds of dishes, a mumble of conversation. A distant giggle. Helen herself barked out a brief laugh. "Not Vegas, sweetie. Reno!" Turns out she had, within the last month, gotten back together with her ex-husband, Theo. "We're married again. Can you believe it! Just like that. Just this morning. Congratulate me?"

When Helen was flustered or excited, her South Carolina childhood started coming through in her vowels. "Just feels like we're meant to be together." *Fuh-eel-uhs*. Long story short, Theo had come back to New York to plead his case. His father had passed away, left him the family business. A Charleston brokerage firm. He wanted to settle down, start a family. "Said he couldn't stop thinking about me. Isn't that just the sweetest thing?"

"Um."

"Reason I'm calling, I've got a moving service all set up to empty out my apartment tomorrow morning, but I can't get hold of my landlord. Won't answer his phone. Could you let them in, do you think?"

Helen, not in New York. Helen, moving on. Tossing off her old life. Chloe, part of that life.

Growing older, Chloe was finding it harder to make friends. Was it age? Didn't matter, really. If Helen was abandoning New York, what did Chloe have left for her in the city? Foreign sales was a young woman's game. How many more trips to Frankfurt could she honestly make? Chloe said to Singer, "I've got some vacation time left. Can I come see you?"

"Sure, yeah. Of course."

Did he sound relieved? Grateful? Maybe she was imagining it? "You sure?"

"God yes."

She hadn't eaten. From the airport they went to a cowboy diner. A late lunch, but it was crowded. "Cattle auction this morning. This is where folks meet up after." A row of ranchers at the counter, thick rounded backs. The smell of grease. Round-cushioned stools fixed to the floor and pies rotating behind glass. They took a booth. A harried waitress threaded her way through with a coffee pot. She touched Singer on the shoulder. "Hey, stranger."

"Lori, this is Chloe. Chloe, Lori."

The waitress handed them menus. "Meetcha. Back in a sec to take your orders."

Chloe studied him. "I like your beard."

He scratched at his chin. "That time of year again." He unfolded a pair of cheap reading glasses. "What do you feel like having?"

"Those glasses are new, too."

He peered at her over their tops. "Getting old is all. What're you having?"

"Oatmeal, I guess. How's Abe doing?"

He folded away his glasses and pulled out a can of chew. "Abe's gone."

"What?"

"Left me last week. After they found Pete's truck."

"Sorry, what? His truck?"

"Remember that Canyon Reservoir, right below where we found them yearlings?"

"The one with the steep sides?"

"Yeah. Down in there. Somebody drove that truck right out into the middle of it. There were some hunters flying around, looking for elk. This dry weather, that reservoir was drawn down so low the tires were showing."

"Were you surprised to see it in there?"

"Goddamn elk hunters . . ."

She let the question sit there. Then: "How'd they get it out?"

"Brought one of the county's dozers in there, a D9. Took about a hundred yards of chain."

She could see it perfectly. The yellow dozer, the slip of its iron treads, the rocking, reluctant release of the truck. "That must have been quite the spectacle."

"You bet." He was pleased that she'd consider the aesthetics of it. "Like hauling up a dinosaur."

"So then Abe left the ranch?"

"Yep."

"Because you knew about that truck being there?"

He picked up the menu again. "I'm changing my mind. That biscuits and gravy is looking pretty good."

An hour into the drive, he had his arm across the back of the seat, not quite touching her shoulder. How do you say *codependence* in French? How do you say, *any port in the storm?* Close to his ranch, speeding too fast around a curve, they came close to hitting another truck. In their lane, traveling the opposite direction. Singer jerked the wheel hard. For one suspended moment, they were eye-to-eye with the driver. A young man in a flat-brimmed cowboy hat and red scarf. She briefly found him handsome. But he was already flipping them off, middle finger out held flat against the windshield. A furious scowl. Then he was gone.

"Well," she said, looking back for a last glimpse of brake lights, "that was rude."

"Ah that's just Curt."

"Curt Fahler?"

"Cocky little turd. Always was. Reminds me of bull riders. That cocky short man's disease."

"I don't know any bull riders."

"Well, take my word for it. Short man's disease."

That evening, he sat back, sipping hard at the latest in a quick series of screwdrivers. Three to her one. He was wearing shapeless buckskin slippers. "These old feet of mine have just been stepped on one too many times." He positioned the jug of vodka by his chair for quick access. "I'm not from here. That's what it comes down to. Truth is, these folks have just been biding their time, thirty years of biding their time, trying to find some damn thing to pin on me."

She recognized self-pity when she saw it. Shoes off and legs curled up on the couch, one of his red heelers was stretched out with its head on her lap. This was Dante, the friendly one.

She pretended to notice, for the first time, a fiddle hanging over the mantle. "You play?"

"Hell yeah, I play. Wanna hear?" His energy was calculated, self-conscious. He was determined to dodge melancholy.

He limped to the fireplace and took the fiddle off its hooks, lodged it under his bicep, and waved the bow, counting time. When it suited him, he drew the bow across in one long, cat-strangling squeal. Then another. And another. He stomped his foot. One more squeal then he relented, going gentle and slow, a three-note imitation of Philip Glass. It came close to music. "That's about all I know."

"You should take it on the road."

He dropped his fiddle to his side in a posture of exhaustion. He set it back on its hooks and knelt beside her, pushing the dog aside. Her lap was warm from the dog's head. She was wearing jeans, and now he scraped at the denim with his fingernails, looking for a grip. She touched his hair.

He said, his voice muffled by her hip, "Been thinking about what you said."

"What did I say?"

"How you're my last chance."

"When did I say that?"

"You ever think about moving to Montana?"

"You ever think about moving to New York."

He sat back on his heels. "Too many people."

"Not enough people."

"What do you have in New York you couldn't leave behind?"

"A job. What do you have here?"

"History. Where's that leave us?"

She rattled her ice. "Compromise?"

"Hard to imagine what that would look like."

He was still on his knees. A rare vulnerability. She'd never had the opportunity to look down on him like this. Singer. She touched his cheek, ran her fingers around the rasp of his chin. "I wish . . ."

"What."

"I wish you'd be honest. Trust me. A little."

He sat back on his heels. Stared at her in the manner of a dog puzzling out a mysterious command. Finally said, "Bullshit."

"Eh?"

"Bullshit. You're looking for excuses. Hedging your bets. You got no reason to believe I've been anything other than honest."

"Ask you a direct question about Pete? You change the subject. Every goddamn time."

"That's not true."

"Okay. So. Did you know about Pete's murder?"

"I helped bury him."

There was so much silence in the room.

He considered her reaction. "See?"

———

Two days later, his wipers beat a slow pulse, rasping against ice and snow. He parked in the drop-off lane at the airport. Said, "I got something for you." From under the seat, he produced his battered briefcase, then a thin sheaf of papers. "I can't wrap my head around the notion of building a proposal, asking to get paid for something I haven't written yet. So I've just been writing." He curled it into a tube, beat it against his leg.

"A memoir?" She almost reached for it, stopped herself.

"The first few chapters is all. I'd be curious for your opinion."

"Okay."

"Chloe . . ."

"Yeah?"

"Thing is. You should know. Right? If it weren't for you. The way everybody's treating me . . ."

"What, Singer?"

"I want to be honest with you. But I don't . . ." He opened the tube of his manuscript and passed it to her where it sat on her knee, slowly opening. "Hell, I'm just a chatterbox, aren't I." This was so out of character. Singer and discomfort. He said, "I'm in a rock and a hard place kind of situation here, to be honest."

She turned to the first page, picked out a phrase at random. *It was so quiet. The squeak of our boots on the snow rose up like nails twisting in boards. We were the first or last men on the earth. Lone survivors of an epidemic, an ice age.* "You start with Buddy? The guy who killed Pete?"

Singer winced. "See, now he's just the guy who killed

Pete. This gets out, Buddy . . . That's the only thing he'll ever be. The guy who killed Pete."

"But that's who it's about."

"And Emma."

"Your sister?"

"Yeah."

The manuscript on her lap. "What are you going to call it?"

The two agents found her in the airport bar, this side of TSA. She had some time to kill. Figured, Bloody Mary? Why the hell not. "Miss Barnes? Mind if we have a seat?" *Heavy* southern accent: vowels with too many syllables. She'd just then tucked away Singer's manuscript into her carry-on grip. Lucky. "I'm sorry. Who are you?" She still had a foot in Singer's world, blinking at snowflakes. The agents must have been biding their time until she was alone. Had they been tailing Singer? Or maybe they had her airline schedule. Post Patriot Act, that information was surely available to the right badge. In any case, they were already pulling out their chairs.

Two agents, but the guy in charge, the man who had spoken, was the more striking of the two. Skinny, and wearing a custom-tailored suit that emphasized the skinniness, dark blue with white stitching around the collar and cuffs. A good six-foot-two. The cowboy boots added another couple inches, the Stetson another six.

His partner was flyover-state cop cliché. A poorly-trimmed mustache. Jowly and judgmental. He crossed his hands over his belly, considering her.

The tall guy flipped open a black leather wallet, laid his badge out on the table. "I'm Glen Sweete, this here's Duane Brackett."

"Okay. Do you mind?" She put her fingers on the badge folder, pulled it toward her. Montana Department of Justice, Investigations Bureau. A photo from a time when Sweete didn't have quite the mileage on him. No bags under the eyes, thinner lines around his mouth.

He said, "Grady Fisk asked us to help out a bit with this one. You met Grady, yeah?"

She closed the wallet, pushed it back toward him. Considered her potential reactions (rude and indignant? obsequious and pandering?), went with mild surprise over a layer of ennui. "What can I help you with, Glen?"

"Now that's what I like to see. Thank you. Polite right out of the gate. I told Duane, I said, she's going to be helpful to us, I can just feel it."

"All right. What can I help you with?"

"We'd like to talk a bit about your friend, there. Eli Singer."

"Okay."

"Yes ma'am. We figure, here's a guy who's been covering up a murder for the last thirty-some years. Hiding it. Which is an offense. Offense against the state, offense against humanity, you ask my opinion. That poor man's family. All these years, not knowing what became of him."

"I'm not sure I can be very helpful after all." Pleasant enough, but with steel in her voice. She was no stranger to cop shows. Interrogation techniques. Good cop, bad cop. Or, in this case, tall cop short cop. They were looking for an eyewitness. She was no fool. She felt umbrage at the notion of being played; also (being honest with herself) a distant flush of power at how she was, at this moment, holding the tiller of Singer's freedom.

"Well, now, see, Duane and me, we were afraid you'd take that tack. So we're hoping we can make a case as to why you should reconsider."

"Well, I don't know anything. He's denied everything. And I believe him."

"But you have your suspicions."

"Well, I'm not sure, I . . ."

"You hired a private investigator."

She sat back. "So much for client privilege."

He made a regretful moue. "Doesn't exist. Not unless you hired him through an attorney. Usually, the private guys will resist, but you stepped on old Jackson's toes a bit, so he was pleased to be forthcoming."

"It's all circumstantial. All of it. And I trust Singer. He's a good man. He is."

"Good men do bad things. Happens all the time." Sweete crossed his legs, put his cowboy hat over the knee. He touched the brim of it, ran his fingers along the sharp edge. "Mostly what Duane and me wanted to tell you, wanted to make sure you knew how it's a crime to be helping him along. Accessory after the fact. If you know something and you don't pass it along to law enforcement? You're in trouble right there with him, ma'am. Jail sentence kind of trouble."

"Well, like I said, I don't know anything." Stare straight ahead, Chloe. Do not, do not glance at your bag.

"All right." He nodded agreeably. "That's just fine, then. But here's my card. Duane, you got a business card for Miss

Barnes here? Okay, here you go then. Tuck these away. If you change your mind, or he gets to be more forthcoming on down the road, I want you to give us a call, hear? Be doing yourself a favor, ma'am. I'm just being honest now."

"I appreciate it." She brought the cards together, evened them up in her fingers. "If you don't mind, I got a plane to catch."

"Sure enough." They both stood, and Sweete carefully set his hat on his head, squared it up. "Safe travels. Give us a call, you hear?"

"I hear."

Homestead Cabins

Salted through alee
of windswept
ridgelines, you see them
tucked into coulees,
slumping soft as
sponges. All the little
lost and long gone lives
somehow lingering still,
a son, a father, a wife
a daughter, whispering
in their private language
of sighs, the soft, sibilant
winds of regret.

IT WAS QUITE A spectacle. The resurrection of Pete's truck. Abe and me stood on a bluff above the reservoir, watching the D9 churn slowly back, listening to the heavy tow chain ping and chirp as the metal drew tight. Grady Fisk and his deputy stood down there beside it, overseeing the work. Too close to be safe, my opinion. If that chain decided to break, it could send somebody to the hospital. Dylan Marney drove the cat, and another dozen or so citizens of Garfield County stood further around on the rim, stomping against the cold. Curt Fahler wasn't welcome on my property but I noted a couple of Curt's cousins on his mother's side. We had Dylan's people from down on the Musselshell, a few of those Flannerys from over on Sand Springs. I guess they'd been staying with the Marneys. This was grist for the gossip mill such as rarely comes along in Garfield County. Once word got out, who'd want to miss it?

There was a skim of early-November ice on the water, and as the rotted tires of Pete's truck rocked slightly within the ice, we all heard an enormous, distant sound of crumpling paper. The water under the ice bloomed up black, flattening and spreading against the translucent ceiling. The cat's engine hit a higher note, and the truck was, all in a moment, released. Birthed from the mud and ice to rock upside down on the bank, shedding curtains of water. The doors wore scabrous chunks of clay.

Abe stood considering Pete's truck, then the dozer, then me. Abe, who had spent his entire working life on this ranch. He'd been uncharacteristically silent of late. We'd been eating our breakfasts together with no more than a word or two passed between us. He had no other home to speak of, precious little family. But seeing this truck, the physical evidence of Buddy's duplicity, he was forced to consider the notion that his world might not be the stable place he'd believed it to be. He found his red cloth handkerchief, blew his nose. Touched his eyes, rheumy in the cold breeze. Finally said, "Eli? You didn't know nothing about this?" He put a pleading, upturned hitch on the question. His wind-chapped cheeks, his pale hair light as dandelion fluff.

Probably I should have lied to him. *Continued* to lie. There are times, I've told myself, when lies serve a purpose. But I was exhausted by it all. "I knew it was down there, yeah."

"You been playing me for a fool?"

"No, Abe. No. *Protecting* you. Trying to protect you is all." I reached for his shoulder.

He dodged my hand, stepping back. "So Buddy? Buddy killed Pete? And you knew about it? All these years you knew about it. All these *years*?"

Below us, out of earshot, Grady Fisk, in his slicker and galoshes, had wrenched open a door. Stepped back from the wash of water. He had a digital camera, and started taking photos. A quick wink of the flash.

"Buddy always tried to do the right thing, Abe," I said.

Abe's mouth turned up in a sad, stressful moue. His cheeks had gone wet. "So he did it then, didn't he. Killed old Pete."

I was doing this. Me. To Abe. "He's the one drove Pete's truck into the reservoir."

"All these years, you been lying to me."

I couldn't admit to it. Couldn't deny it.

He blinked hard, cleared his throat. Looked past me at the horizon. "So what do I do now, Eli? Tell me that. What the hell am I supposed to do now?"

"We do what we've got to. Same as always."

Buddy had, at times, both a dearth and an excess of empathy. It made him awkward in certain situations. The notion that a conversation might be effortless, that a person could enjoy it, was foreign to him. He kept a notebook in his shirt pocket. A small reporter's pad, it fit easily within the horizon of his big hand. From a distance, maybe he was writing into his cupped paw. His to-do notebook. It came out half a dozen times a day for a verb, a noun. "Buy seed, fix pump." But he also wrote down what might have otherwise, in a normal man, passed for the openings of a conversation. "Julia. Pretty blue hat." Or, "Walter. Good-looking bulls." I once read, "Eli. Do better." I performed for his approval. Usually he withheld it. In this way, and in this way only, he was a cruel man.

That fall my sister and I attended the one-room schoolhouse on the top of the hill. Seven miles away, it sat perched on that meridian where the flat farm ground crumbled away to timbered coulees. A doublewide trailer, partitioned into halves, served as our classroom. The teacher, Ms. Norton, was a petite woman, and blunt-spoken. We liked her. She wore her hair short and drove a motorcycle, a little Honda 90. The school board let her live in the back half of the trailer for free.

There were eight students, including Emma and me. Lyn Hagerton, ten years old, was a fat, pale boy with thumb-smeared glasses. Now he's a withdrawn, arthritic sheep rancher west out of Crooked Creek. Sheep rather than his father's cattle, and there are some at church who still refuse to sit in the same pew. Debbie Weaver married Dwight Duncan and nearly died of peritonitis birthing their second child. Shelly Bowers, a duplicate of her mother (right down to the wad of Copenhagen), married Sherman Boyd but left him for a carpet salesman out of Miles City. Freddy Whitman, already so good at math that Ms. Norton was steering him through an algebra textbook, discovered first gin and then methamphetamine, eventually to die of AIDS in a Seattle flophouse.

Apart from Emma, the only other student in eighth grade was a boy named Martin Miller. He would eventually marry an Assiniboin woman from Wolf Point and open a convenience store. Heavy-jowled now, and hips wide as a woman's, as a teenager he'd been skinny as sticks, unbeatable at basketball. He was also infatuated from the start with Emma. When she ignored him, Martin's nervous courtesy gave way to puzzlement, finally to resentment.

The day of my fistfight with Martin, I remember an early snowman going lopsided under the basketball hoop, Emma reading a book on the school steps, and Martin spinning a basketball on his finger. There was a group of us around him. He said (to no one in particular), "Look at that little prissy-pants. Trying to pretend like she ain't the biggest whore in Montana."

I didn't know it was in me, this sudden anger. I charged at
him. He shoved me away. "What's *your* problem?" I lost my feet,
then charged him again, my head between his knees. I lifted
him off the ground. "Sonofabitch! Sonofabitch!" I was punching at his ribs. Having been hit once or twice in the solar plexus,
I had the idea that this was where you went to hurt somebody.
My fists bounced off his coat. He rolled over, trapping me with
his knees. "Hold on Eli, just hold on a second." I twisted free.
My fist found his cheek, hard enough to skin my knuckles. And
now he was punching back. My eye, my nose. I had much the
worst of it. Nevertheless, I was the one they had to pull away.
Sobbing, "He called her a whore! He called her a whore!"

"Harder," Buddy said. "This ain't no game." I cocked my elbow
and punched him in the sternum. The cushion of his coat, the
hard sting of a metal button against my knuckle. He rocked
back on his knees. "Use your shoulder, use your weight." I hit
him again. "Pretend like this button is my nose. Always try to
hit them in the nose."

"I'm *try*ing."

"You're not." He took my shoulders and shoved me back,
sending me sprawling flat. "Get mad." He inched forward on
his knees, then shoved me down again. "Mad, I said." Crying
with frustration, I lunged up off the ground, swinging blindly.
His cheekbone popped on my knuckle. He ducked away. My
forearms were clubbing against his ears, his cheeks. Then he
was hugging me, folding me into his big arms: "Okay. Okay.
Okay. Good job. Okay, that's good." At the window, watching us, my mother.

I stepped away from him, breathing hard. Finally said, "Okay. Okay."

"We're family. Family sticks together." He grabbed me again, roughly and inexpertly under one arm. The rough warmth of his canvas jacket. "You did the right thing, punching that little turd, even if he got the best of it. What I'm saying, you did good, boy."

Was he proud? He hadn't used that word, but maybe I could take it as a given. It was a small thing, of course—Buddy being proud of me—but nothing grows so well as a small thing when it's carved into a young heart. But this fine moment, like all vivid memories, is colored now through the lens of subsequent, poisonous events. There was also, it seems to me now, under the satisfaction, a certain foreboding. A presentiment. Having found a moment that I would like to keep, an instant with Buddy within which I'd like to live, I now had something that could be taken away from me. I had a sense, despite myself, for the many ways this could go wrong.

Autumn proceeded apace. Cottonwoods shed their yellow leaves. We gathered cows and loaded them into semis. Saw the trucks pull away, one after the other. There was the near-daily mutter of the chainsaw, the hollow chunk of firewood stacked into a pile. And my sister began her slow transformation. She was already less the frazzled, frenetic teenager and more the poised (albeit uncertain) woman. She held herself with self-conscious composure, a stack of imagined books flat on her head. Cottage cheese and peaches for dinner, hairpins in her lips as she stood before the mirror. After the wedding, she took over Mother's old room. She subscribed to half a dozen fashion magazines. A few evenings a week, she rode Buddy's colts around the corral. She'd given them her own names—Banjo, Pierre, Orlando—and talked about them as if they were people: "That little pinto filly is just so stubborn, but her heart's in the right place." The older colts she would take out into the ranch, trotting the long bare ridges down toward the lake. I'm sure she found a sense of adventure and pleasure in this, not least for leaving us behind.

From cleaning their houses she knew the neighbors and passed along the gossip. "Those Cunninghams make good money off their sorghum, but the family's just all mortgaged out on equipment. You should hear how they argue." But gossip, of course, goes both ways. And as word spread about her and Pete, as whispers stacked up into rumors, as rumors reached a critical density and tipped over into conclusions, she began to lose her housekeeping work. Vindictiveness has its satisfactions. I remember her carrying Mother's vacuum to the car, awkward in the embrace of the corrugated tentacles (cheerful and humming), only to return half an hour later, dumping everything in a pile on the porch. "Emma?" She rushed past me to her room, slamming the door.

Eventually, she was only cleaning Pete's house. "I thought Pete was broke."

"He told me he'd never had a prettier housekeeper. Says I'm about the prettiest girl he's ever seen."

"Geez, Emma. You know how old he is?"

"You should see your face right about now."

"*Emma.*"

She shook back her hair to show me her profile. "You don't think I'm pretty?" She had been braiding her hair, but now it hung loose. The waves clung to her cheeks. "Am I getting a little fat?" She slapped the corner of her thigh.

"A little bit, yeah."

"Bullshit. Really?"

"Nah. I think you're real pretty. Of course you're pretty."

She unwrapped a stick of gum and folded it into her mouth. "Yeah, I know."

Defending my sister, I said to Buddy, "These yokels don't know a good thing when they see it."

"You're not old enough for scorn. It don't suit you."

Pete was a packrat, a beachcomber, a pawn shop parvenu. It must have been later in November of that year—there was snow on the ground—when I went with Emma to his house. I remember a tower of hubcaps behind his couch and, on his mantel, a menagerie of ceramic figurines. By the fireplace, a nude Asian couple locked in coitus (to my delight, you could move the parts back and forth). One spare bedroom given over entirely to old newspapers. Thousands of them, stacked in columns. "Goes back to 1951. See I had me an idea. Newspapers as souvenirs. Wait a few more years then start selling folks papers from the day they was born, day they was married. Cost me fifty cents and a few new floor joists, I sell them back for twenty dollars each, maybe thirty. What do you think?"

"You must be pretty smart, reading all these papers."

"Hell, I don't read them. That would lessen the market value. Like driving a new car off the lot."

Emma clattered a bucket through the front door, hauling in Mother's vacuum. Pete said, "Now, I sell off all these collections along with my ranch, put them like a cherry on top, I'll have enough to retire down in that Cabo San Lucas. Buy me a little aluminum ponga, fish for tuna, marlin, whatever. Never have to work another day."

Emma was filling her bucket at the kitchen sink. "Paris," she called back, "like I been saying."

"Margueritas and Mamaseetas. Piña coladas and Pappa may I."

She struggled past us with the bucket. "Paris. Bonjour, aloha." She threw back the cotton sheet Pete used for a bedroom door. "Don't laugh, Mr. Fahler. Rate I'm going, I'll have me a plane ticket." She snapped her fingers. "Like that."

"Oh, I know you will." He snapped his fingers. "Like that. What I want to know," he nudged me, "will there be any rugs to Hoover over there?"

She stuck out her tongue at him, then turned from us, bent over the vacuum.

Pete stared at her, his expression that of a man trapped down in a well, blinking up at the light. Emma lingered over the hose attachment.

Pete shook himself awake, snapping his fingers, "Just like that."

What did my sister see in him? God knows. Maybe it was simple animal attraction. But what animal willingly pairs with the geriatric? And Pete himself. What was there in him, or what was missing in him, that made him capable of pursuing my sister? What monstrous twist in his circuitry allowed him to take his own moral compass, distorted though it was, and just toss it clean out the window. Perhaps most importantly, what was there in us, the rest of us—her family, our community—that tacitly allowed it?

He'd married Matty, his wife, when she wasn't all that much older than Emma. Seventeen. But consider the gulf of those three years. They'd met at a cake raffle near Brusett. Who was that cutie bringing in the noodle salad? "Last time I seen you, you were arguing over a Barbie doll with your sister." He convinced Matty away for a giggling, spit-filled kiss behind the barn, and six months later, they were married. The mother complained about Pete's age but the father was heard to argue on Pete's behalf. "Hell, he's got his own ranch."

Matty had never heard about blow jobs but she knew accounting. She could keep his ranch books. She decided they could afford at least a couple of kids. A girl, then a boy. A doctor said, with regret, that their little girl wasn't right. Hundred-and-fifty bucks to tell them what they already knew. This child who sat for hours giggling at moths around a light bulb, who ate glitter by the fistful, who squatted in the living room to shit her pants.

He woke one morning with an itchy walnut for a prostate and the smell of bacon in his bedclothes and the realization that he was forty-five years old. Christ. And what did he have to show for it? Maybe a divorce would make things better. But then, no. Turns out, not so much. Nobody's an alcoholic who just drinks beer. But then hell, whiskey's not nearly so fattening. Every day felt like a fresh parenthesis, an ellipses, a pair of dashes where his real life was supposed to be.

Matty took the kids and moved into Jordan. Started bartending. She developed a taste for crème de menthe and

Camels. I met her once. So thin you could see the threads of muscle working in her arms, she stank of a certain kind of sexual arrogance. Before Pete's disappearance, before his death, Matty was determined to take on the care of their daughter, Nora. The poor child. Sweet-tempered and obese, weak eyes warped behind thick spectacles, when I met her she stood sweating in a Forty-Niners sweatshirt that she would allow no one to take away from her. Emma knelt before the girl. "So what was that you were watching back there? Bugs Bunny?"

"Ugs!" Nora's round-moon face split in a grin. "Ugs!" She held two fingers to her temples and hopped around in a circle, shaking the floor. "Ugs! Ugs! Ugs!"

Curt was six years old and obsessed with toy trucks. I found him in a backyard sandbox. "What you got there? Tonkas?" He squinted up at me from under the brim of a sombrero-sized straw cowboy hat. "John Deere end loader and scraper." He held it up. "This one here's a Case Farmall. Comes with a brush hog but I don't know where that's at. And this one's a Massey Ferguson." He bent back to his work. Through the open window, I could hear Matty go plaintive. "Honey, you should move back in here with us. The kids miss you. Or how about this, how about we move back in there with you? Let it be like it was? You looked so handsome coming through the door today. Didn't he, Emma? Looked so handsome."

Pete's heifers arrived in early December. Half a dozen stock trucks pulled into Buddy's winter pasture, tires crunching at frozen mud. Ramps were pulled out, doors opened. The drivers each climbed up on the slatted sides of their trailers, punching cattle prods through the slats, zapping haunches, ribcages. The heifers startled and reared, jumped out kicking and bucking.

As opposed to his own older mother cows, which could largely fend for themselves, these first-calf heifers needed extra care. Buddy felt the responsibility. These weren't his cows, after all. Feeding became our morning ritual. We used his old flatbed. A spare tire and handyman roped up against the cab, doors belled in by scratching cattle, the engine consistently leaked half a quart of oil a week. The shifter on the steering column and an AM radio tuned to a country station out of Miles City. For better reception, he'd fashioned an antenna extension out of welded rebar, and as he drove the rusted arms of it bounced like a conductor's baton. "Momma, don't let, your babies, grow up, to be cowboys. I sing good, huh?"

"Like a meadowlark."

"You must not a heard many meadowlarks."

I used his town truck to tow it around the pasture while he popped the clutch behind, slewing both vehicles to the side. Feeding, he would idle us along while I stood balanced on the bed, kicking out bales. Pete's heifers gathered in a line behind us. Afterward, he would park the truck to smoke a cigarette and study the feeding cows. I stood by his door, resting a gloved hand on the mirror. He said, "There's a few of them didn't take. Too skinny."

"Is that bad?"

"Always a few. Reason why you preg test." He flicked his ash. "Should've caught them before they shipped them up here. But hell, Pete ain't feeding them. No skin off his back."

"When are they going to start calving?"

"Another few months. February, I guess." He saw that I was worried about it. "You won't have to do much. Just keep an eye out late at night."

"Okay."

We studied the cows. He said, "How we doing, son?"

"We going to have enough hay?"

"No, I mean, you liking the way things are?"

"Sure. Yeah, I guess."

"Me too."

Cows feeding, a boy whom he'd just called son, a little money in the bank. "Funny," he said, "how a guy makes a thousand decisions every day, then he fills out some little want ad, some little half inch of newspaper, and everything changes. It's like taking some sort of pill or something. A pill that lasts your whole life."

"You think they make a pill for sisters?"

"Ah hell, Emma's all right."

"You sure?"

"You don't think so?"

"No, no. Yeah, she's fine."

"All those little decisions. Hell, you think about it enough," he tossed the cigarette away, "makes you scared to step out the front door."

We'd had snowstorms, yes; intimations of winter, but the night winter came for true, you could feel moisture in the wind. Buddy, usually so chary about predicting the weather, stamped into the kitchen. "Heavy snow by morning." He hugged Mother at the sink, tilting his face into her neck. "We always had popcorn with the first big snow. What do you think, Bess? Feel like some popcorn?"

He brought out the Monopoly board out and started dividing cash into piles. "Eli? You want to be the little dog, or maybe the car? I'm always the hat." Emma sat cross-legged on the floor, working one of Buddy's puzzles. The Empire State Building in Warhol fluorescents. It took up one whole corner of the room. Buddy said, "What do you think Emma? You a schnauzer kind of gal?"

"I'm actually a little tired."

"You look like a schnauzer gal to me." He gave the dice a practice roll.

She stood, yawning theatrically. "No, I guess, no thanks. Guess I'll get on to bed."

Mother came from the kitchen with a bowl of popcorn. "You aren't getting sick are you?" She moved to feel Emma's forehead.

"I'm *fine*, Mom. Just tired."

Mom said to Buddy, "We can play just the three of us?"

I heard her leave the house. The thump of her heels, the creak of the door. One o'clock in the morning.

It took me a few minutes to find my pants, my shirt. Outside, it was unexpectedly bright. A full moon behind clouds threw out a blue, diffuse light. I caught a glimpse of Emma as she led her horse away from the barn. Patches, by its piebald markings. She swung onto his back and trotted out of the yard, hugging his neck for the warmth. The other horses were still in their stalls, feeding on the grain Emma had fed out. She was always a soft touch.

I threw a halter around a gelding named Cactus, wrestled a saddle over his back. "Where the hell is she going, you suppose?" She'd left tracks in the snow, conspicuous as a series of postholes. Cactus was invigorated by the novelty of it all. Riding through a blizzard at night. He kept wanting to play, veering away from Emma's trail to dig at the drifts. The moon drew humped constellations from every bowed branch, each round-capped stump. I said, "Maybe she's just taking one of her nighttime rides." But then she turned off into the Breaks. "She'd never go this way, given a choice." Her saddle had been left hanging in the barn, so she was riding bareback. Was she compelled by an image? The romance of it? In the absence of a wild moor, a snowstorm would do; instead of Heathcliff, how about Pete Fahler. The girl on a horse, riding toward her lover.

Drawing close to Pete's house, his yardlight gave off an unfocused yellow corona. She'd be putting the horse in his barn about now. One hundred yards or more from the barn to the house, and she'd probably run a little, the horse's heat between her thighs diminishing. He'd be waiting. Coming together, he'd swing her around, kiss her cheek. After a few turns, he'd let her drop, grab at his back. "Jesus. Yowch." She'd picked up a cold somewhere, and when he first kissed her she tilted her head away for a sneeze. He kissed her nose. She loved it that he kissed her nose. "My little Emma."

She'd brush past him, anxious for the warm stove. Less certain now, surely. Snow, lover, horse, but it didn't work so well in here. His house smelled, despite her cleaning. Coffee in a cracked, Seattle Expo mug and a piece of store-bought pie on a pewter plate. These were his rituals of courtship. Standing for the walk into the bedroom, he'd already be pulling off his shirt, unbuttoning his pants.

Maybe this was how it went. All I know for certain is what I saw through the window. Their limbs unpieced by the mullion panes, warped into watery waves by old glass, her bare legs, his hairy ass, working. I had been told about the mechanics of it, this act, but never seen it firsthand. My sister's knee, the wrinkled corner of her hip. There was a little hair on her lower legs, just above the ankles. God, Emma. This man, this place.

Standing outside and staring in, my breath kept wanting to fog up the glass. Cactus breathed green hay into my ear. I twitched him away and, insulted, he pushed his nose against my back, knocking me against the window. My forehead thumped against glass. Pete was too preoccupied to notice, but Emma glanced up, startled. Me. Little Eli. Chin and nose, fingers splayed white at the tips. She glanced at Pete (his ear, his face in the pillow) then tilted her head back, studying the room as if from my eyes.

She came back around to me, smiling.

They decided to spend Christmas in New York. "Nothing like the city in December, Singer. Most romantic place on earth." The day before his arrival, a bouquet of three dozen pink and red roses appeared on her desk. Her first thought, of course, was Singer. Very sweet. Out of character, but sweet. Instead, the note read, "Forgive me? XOXO Richard."

She put her nose in. Thirty-six. You could never accuse Richard of half measures. And she hadn't received flowers in . . . Jesus, years. Just years. Richard (never Rich, or Richie, or Dick—emphatically always Richard) was that cocky, well-dressed prick who'd expected her to sit still for his tryst to Milan. She was onboard for Singer, of course. But nice to know there were options on the table.

There were things tourists did in New York—she'd prepared a list—but Singer had his own ideas. "Bill Charlap's at the Village Vanguard. You mind?" He'd come off the plane with a swollen eye going black, a split lip that kept cracking and leaking fluid when he smiled.

"What's with the . . . ?" She touched her own lip.

"Aw hell. Ran into Curt Fahler a few days ago." A scab on the largest knuckle of his right hand.

"Did you get the best of him?"

"What do you think?"

Either he was oblivious to the damage reticence could inflict (trust a girl, Singer), or he just didn't give a shit. They came to sit knee to knee in the club's subterranean belly. Low ceilings, the floor rumbling with the intestinal passing of trains. She'd been looking forward to Singer's visit but he was already somewhere else. Two-drink minimum, and she went through her glasses of Pinot Grigio in ten minutes. She didn't need this crap. She raised a hand for another one. She thought about the roses on her desk at the office. Should she text Richard? It would be rude not to, not to at least say thanks.

Then the show started, and the roses, Richard, her Singer-anxiety, it all went away. Charlap was soft-spoken, balding, rumpled. He might have been an adjunct professor, ego shattered by one too many professional setbacks. But put him at the piano, his hands were butterflies considering the keys. One of those musicians who seems only a vector for talent. Afterward, she said, "Thanks, Singer. Seriously, thank you."

He might have been a little smug. Two in the morning, but some of the magic still lingered, an echo of Gershwin in the walls. "Buddy would have killed to be here. The Village Vanguard, man. I got an Ahmad Jamal record, you can hear the trains in the background. Buddy and jazz. You knew about that, right?" He caught her expression. "Sorry. Bad choice of words. Killed to be here."

"So yeah. Speaking of which, I read your chapters."

"I've rewritten a bit since then."

"What I'm wondering, you have a lawyer?" She had been weighing whether or not to tell Singer about Sweete. Did Singer know that the Garfield County sheriff had been sent to the showers? Would it *change* anything? Plusses and minuses, she'd finally decided there was little reason to worry him. It was out of their hands. But he *could* do at least one thing for himself.

"That's all you've got to say about it?" A brittle smile. "I need a lawyer." The artist's ego, offended.

"No, I mean, it's lovely. You're a poet, of course, but. Singer."

"I'm not spending money on a lawyer."

"Of *course* you need a lawyer. Once this gets out, after other people read this thing . . ."

"*You're* my reader."

"That's sweet, but . . . what?"

"I'm not writing this for publication. I've decided. Far as I'm concerned, I just need one reader." He reached out a slightly-crooked finger. Touched her gently on the sternum. "One."

An author who wasn't interested in selling his work. "Leslie said an auction would . . ."

"I sold off my mother cows. Did I tell you?"

"I'm not sure what that means."

"Means that as of about three weeks ago I'm fresh out of the ranching business. And it means I got some money in the bank."

Around them, the Vanguard staff was turning chairs up on tables. The maître d' pushed a broom by the stage.

Singer found his can of Skoal. "Should we go?"

She sat back, digesting it. Singer, not a rancher. "So, why?"

"If Curt comes after my ranch, I don't want him to get every damn thing. I haven't seen papers yet, haven't been served, so I can still sort of divest myself of assets. That's what I did. Divested some assets. Drinks are on me." He tossed a couple of twenties on the table. Reached around for her coat, held it up for her. "Abe gone, I can't run the place anyway. Sell it now, sell it later."

She let him drape her coat around her.

Singer, not a rancher. A poet, full stop. It disturbed her, and for no real reason she could say. Who was he now, this man beside her? To cover her confusion, she went for solicitude. "And so how are you doing? Are you okay with it? Not being a rancher?"

"Talk to me here in a few months."

The next day was gray and cold, threatening snow. "You ever been ice skating, Singer?"

Not since he was a kid. "We used to have these skates mail-ordered from Sears-Roebuck." They stepped awkwardly onto the ice of Trump Rink, teetering, grabbing at each other's arms, layered round with sweaters and long johns, their ankles loose, unstable. Chloe soon caught the trick of it again, and pushed off into long, sweeping glides. Singer tottered in small steps, hands held out like an old man reaching for his walker. The crowd flowed around him. Six-year-olds shot him dirty looks. "Hey, Singer!" She turned briefly backward, shaking her rump to a rhythm. "I'm thinking I should go join the Ice Capades, what do you think?"

He tried walking on his toes. "I'm thinking you got the best pair of skates."

When she came back to him, gliding in a slow circle, he snatched at her arm. They tumbled together, tangled. "Oh, shit. Oww."

He was not one for exhibitions of casual affection. Out of the bedroom, had he ever initiated a kiss? But now, face to face, entangled, he took the tip of his mitten in his teeth and bared his hand. He cupped her cheek in his palm, touched her dripping nose. At this moment, she was precisely where she wanted to be. Their bodies, insulated, removed by layers of cotton and wool, nevertheless aligned themselves in the way of obvious puzzle pieces.

He said, "You're saving my life. You know that, right?"

That night, lying next to him, listening to his soft breathing, she thought, What's a thirty-year-old crime, more or less? Malaria, Ebola, typhoid. Genocide, the drug wars, child abuse. More people had died—innocent people, valued human beings—while she'd been staring at the ceiling than she would likely meet in her lifetime. Boil it down, how did Singer's responsibility for Fahler change the world?

Maybe her first responsibility was to herself. She *needed* this. And Singer needed her, she was almost certain. That goddamn Glen Sweete, who did he think he was?

And what about *her*. Who was looking out for her in this world? Since her father died, who was on her side? No one, no one.

Until now.

She reached for one of his hands and held it loosely between hers. Falling asleep, she gravitated toward his warmth.

This is mine, she thought. *Mine.*

Dear C,

I met a wolf
at the bar
last night.
Rheumy-eyed,
half his teeth,
kicked loose, he
lapped at a saucer
of bourbon
cigarette smoldering
between his first
two toes.
These new ones,
he said,
these packs down
from Canada,
they don't know
nothing but
run, kill, eat,
fuck. But they'll
learn by god,
they'll learn.
He coughed
and shook
his heavy head.
The best elk
are all et up.

Since we parted
it's grown
colder. Do you
remember
our music?
As we sat
on small chairs
during one perfect
riff after another
I took your hand.
and felt so
sorry for that other
me, the
poor toothless
sonofabitch
on the other
side of the
world, the one who
failed to meet you,
who wasn't in
New York
last year
too broke or
too tired,
the other me
who lives
now so little,
and so alone.

SLEEP WAS IMPOSSIBLE. I closed my eyes and here was Pete's ass, working. I turned on the reading lamp, dug out one of Buddy's crosswords. How long had this been going on? The secrecy was surely part of the attraction. Girls liked a secret. I drew a portrait of Pete across the puzzle pattern. Horns, a forked tongue, dripping knife in his head.

An hour later, I heard Emma slip back into the house. The soft squeak of the door. I lunged to turn off my lamp. She stood outside my door, breathing. The door creaked open. "I saw your light." She stepped into the room. She was wearing an unfamiliar shirt. It hadn't been buttoned properly, the collar crooked around her neck.

"Get out."

"You won't tell, will you?"

"I guess Martin was right, huh?"

"I'm not a whore."

"So this is why you've been losing your housekeeping jobs, I guess. Everybody knows but us?"

She shrugged. It was unimportant to her.

"You ever think about what Buddy's going to say?"

"I don't care what Buddy says."

"What about Mom?"

She snorted. Yeah, right.

"What about me?"

"Oh, Eli." She touched the blanket beside my knee.

"Get away."

"You worry too much about what Buddy thinks. Some point, you're going to have to start thinking for yourself."

"I got no idea what you're talking about."

"Got no idea. That's something Buddy would say, isn't it?" Her best defense had always been an attack. "Shut up."

"Are you going to keep my secret?"

"Maybe."

Even I could hear my uncertainty. Emma held out her hand. "Shake on it?"

"I said maybe."

"C'mon. Shake on it?"

Finally, she knew me better than I knew myself. I shook on it.

The days were cold, the house impossible to warm. A chill crept up from the foundation. Walking from bed to bureau, the soles of my bare feet stuck to the floor. Two stoves burned hot but still weren't enough to keep the windows free from frost. The night it dropped to thirty-five below, Buddy turned on all the taps, trickling water through the pipes. Mornings he brushed off the woodpile, filled the kindling box. He returned to the kitchen to sit with coffee. In part because his presence made her nervous, Mother had taken to cooking elaborate breakfasts. Deer sausage and pancakes, eggs and sliced potatoes. Out on the ranch, Buddy would touch his stomach, complaining happily about his bowels. "Hope I don't have to take a shit out in the snow again." In the hour before school, I would help him break out the home place reservoir, watch the cows jostle toward the open water. Buddy said, "Makes you feel needed, don't it?"

For Christmas, he cut a small ponderosa; produced a cardboard box full of tarnished bulbs and snowflake doilies. He tried very hard to create an occasion. Bing Crosby sang "Jingle Bells" while Buddy, placing the decorations, spouted false bonhomie. "What's your favorite part of Christmas there, Eli? Me, I like the smell of a Christmas tree. Emma, what are you hoping for from Santa this year?" Mother could feel that something was wrong—her gaze kept going between me and Emma—but she was lately rather too absorbed in her own climate to pursue it.

That evening, Emma found me alone, sitting against the wall, staring at the tree's blinking lights, scratching at Tony's collar, playing with his ears.

She slid down beside me. "Hey Eli."

"Hey."

"I've been wanting to say thanks. Thanks for keeping a secret."

"Okay."

"Okay, what?"

"Okay, you said it."

She considered me. "You know what Pete told me the other day? Said that I don't belong here. Wasn't that nice? He calls me his Russian princess. Tzarina. I guess that's a real word. Says he sees me at a ballet, drinking champagne." Emma needed a confidante, and had willfully misinterpreted my silence as approval, as collusion. She went on to tell me, without prompting, how Pete was so superstitious, couldn't stand the thought of broken mirrors, black cats, spilled salt. When he was a boy, he'd wanted to be a trapper in Alaska. He loved his children and felt sorry for his ex-wife. "But oh that Matty's just a witch. You wouldn't believe some of the things she makes him do." He kept a back scrubber hung over his showerhead and a pistol under his mattress and it embarrassed him to be seen setting out milk for his barn cats.

"How long you been going over there, anyway."

"Few weeks?"

"How much longer you going to keep going over there?"

"You know what he told me? Said I was a born horse trainer. Said one of these days we might raise quarter horses."

"He's so old, Emma."

"Pete says a person's age is all in their head. He says I'm one of the most mature women he's ever met."

"Pete's a born liar, is what Buddy says."

"Pete says Buddy's just jealous. Said they were best friends until he married Matty."

"He cheated Buddy out of that property."

"Well, Pete talks about how Buddy asked Matty out a time or two. You didn't know that, did you? How Buddy was calling Matty all the time. Wouldn't leave her alone."

"Well."

"Anyway, it doesn't matter. They're friends now. Pete's so relieved. He's really very tender about things like that."

"I thought you wanted to go to Paris?"

"Yeah, right. Like I could ever speak French."

———

For Mother's birthday, in November, Buddy had given her a peach-colored, quilted dressing gown. "Keep you warm on a cold night." A month later, we never saw her in anything else. The brief, twenty-five watt swing of the sub-arctic sun, the long crystalline nights, she found it such an effort to get dressed. Buddy said, "I'm glad you're liking that robe so much."

Buddy had found an old tennis visor. Playing Monopoly, he wore it like a bank teller, shuffling the chance cards until they were broken and loose, rearranging his money, blowing into his dice. Talking like a carnival hawker: "Come on now, big numbers, big numbers that's what I like to see, double fives, okay now. That puts me on . . . Park Place. Whoowhee. Might just own the whole board."

After deigning to join us—"Does it have to be Mo*nop*oly?"—Emma threw herself into the game with avidity, hovering over the board, elbows on her knees, bouncing. "Look at Eli's tiny little bankroll. Hey Buddy, anything in the rules about charity cases? Does the bank have a welfare program?" Mother stared out the window, twirling a rope of hair. "Oh, is it my turn?" We helped her count her cash. "No, that's Buddy's property, Mom. You owe him, what's it say there Buddy, two-fifty." Emma hopped her schnauzer hard down the board, clapping and spinning. "Oh, yeah!"

I went bust the fourth night. Emma counted out the squares. I slid my car down the board. She said, teasing, "Vrooooom." Wordlessly, I handed her the rest of my money. Mother had quit the day before, splitting her cash between the three of us. She sat now off to one side smoking a cigarette, ashtray on her lap. Buddy landed on Broadway. Delighted, Emma reached across to give him a little shove. He said, "Fat lady ain't sung yet, little missy." Later that evening, having beat Buddy as well, Emma kept the metal schnauzer as a souvenir, slipping it furtively into her pocket.

Was it simply pique? Was I so small, so mean-minded? I would like to think now that my betrayal had been for her own good, that I'd had her best interests at heart. Absurd, of course, but pretty to think so.

Sunday afternoons, as part of his weekly routine, Buddy burned that week's trash in a barrel behind the corrals. He poured in a measure of gasoline, tossed a match. Held out his hands, rubbing them together. "Feels good, eh?" He'd been gaining weight with Mother's cooking. Staring down at the fire, his chin tripled.

I held my hands out. "Emma's sure been going over to Pete's a lot."

"Has she?" He seemed unconcerned.

"You haven't noticed?"

"Nope. Fire feels good, don't it."

"It's just, you know. I've been thinking, I probably shouldn't have gotten into that fight with Martin."

"Never a mistake to defend family. I told you that."

"She really is a whore, though."

"Hey. Enough of that."

"She is, though."

"Did you two get in a fight or something?"

"She's sure been going over to Pete's a lot."

I had his attention. "What are you talking about?"

"I promised her I wouldn't tell."

"Tell what?"

"She's been going over to Pete's. A lot."

He rubbed his jowls. "Little Emma."

"Yeah."

"And Pete?"

"I guess. Yeah."

"You think that's why she's been so happy? I thought there for a while it might have something to do with us, with her mother being married and all."

"I don't know. No, I don't think so. Probably Pete."

"Pete Fahler." Buddy glanced at the heifers feeding in the distance. Bemused: "Here I thought *we* were getting the best of *him*."

Buddy liked to talk about the old-timers, how tough they must have been. "Every two foot section of firewood? They had to cut it out with a handsaw. Think about that. A whole winter's worth of firewood sawed out by hand. Think about how much time that took. How much time a chainsaw would have saved. Folks talk about how Colt revolvers tamed the West. No sir, it was Husqvarna and Stihl." For my part, I found few things so frustrating as chopping wood. Heaving up the maul, swinging it around, letting it fall off-center onto the edge of the log. I chopped and chipped and produced nothing but shards and blisters. When Buddy returned from his "heart-to-heart" with Pete, I was halfway through worrying my way around a knotted up chunk of pine. He stood watching. "Chop *through* it."

"I know."

"I know you know."

"What'd Pete have to say?"

"Said he loves her."

"What?"

"Yeah, the damnedest thing. I ain't never heard Pete talk like that. Oh, I'm in love, I love her, blah blah blah. He never even talked about Matty that way."

I swung my maul. It made a hollow, satisfying thunk. "He's a liar you said."

"You know how old Momma was when she married Dad? Fifteen."

"It's not the same. It's *not*. Pete's ugly. He's *old*."

"You got that right. Ugly and old. But he's got his own ranch. Your sister could do worse."

Buddy was missing the point. Whatever the point might be, certainly he was missing it. My sister was two years older than me. And so my first thought, as her younger brother, was never that she was herself too young. Rather: "She's too good for him."

"That's for sure."

Goddamnit.

He did not know Emma, although he thought he did. He did not know my mother. He did not know me.

The day was windless and cold. An inversion had flattened chimney smoke across the roof of the house. Buddy took the maul from me and rolled out a fresh log. "One thing. I don't think we should tell your mother. I don't think that'd be a good idea right about now." He split into the pine with effortless precision. Halves, then quarters. "You want to stack some wood or just stand there watching other people work?"

——

Mondays and Thursdays were my bath days. A cast-iron cradle of lobster-boil, the metal of the tub popping and complaining, the crown of my head touching one end, toes touching the other. I was half asleep when the steam above my head swirled and gathered, funneled toward the door. I jerked a washcloth over my lap. "Geez, Emma!"

"Nothing I haven't seen before." She sat on the toilet seat; considered her reflection in the steam-clogged mirror. "Pete got a visit from Buddy." She picked a box of floss off the sink and spooled out a long rope, winding it around her fingers. "I knew you were going to tell." She twisted the floss into a noose and slipped it over her wrist. "Knew it. Knew you'd be jealous."

"Of *you*?"

"It's just, I was just hoping we could keep things the way they were. At least for a while yet."

Her poise was an insult. I wanted to lunge out, take a swing at her, slap her. I'd been hoping for a tantrum, tears; how could you, how *could* you, that sort of thing. Some demonstration of her affections, something that meant I was still important to her. At the dinner table, she'd been eating with her fork upside down. "Like the Europeans do it." A piece of steak speared on the inverted tines, carrots and peas pushed up. She was doing everything with the awareness of being watched. "It's not going to change anything, you know."

"Will you please leave?"

She tossed the floss into the sink. "Pete's thingamabob is a lot bigger than yours."

———

The ranch in winter was a clock at the end of its wind. The goats still perched mindlessly on their bales but only for a few minutes in afternoon sunlight. The stock pond in front of the house, frozen, had gone quiet as tombs. In the interim between shipping and calving, mother cows lay in the sun chewing cud, waiting. Everything was waiting. Emma stared around and aspired to something more, disdained those of us who were content with the status quo. Aspiration and disdain. How to feel one without the other? She wanted to be better than this, she was better than this.

Pete, assuming that everyone knew about him and Emma, pulled into the yard on a Saturday morning. Honked the horn, reached through his open window to bang the metal of his door, yelling, "Hey Emma. Emmy. Emmma!"

Mother craned her neck out the window. "What's Pete going on about?"

Buddy and I were still at the breakfast table. Buddy with his morning coffee, me with math homework. We exchanged a glance. The front door banged open, and we soon heard Emma's voice mingling with Pete's. No intelligible words but rather tones of clear delight. Laughter. An engine revving, then gravel under tires.

I said, "She's going over to Pete's."

"What for?"

"He's her boyfriend."

"Oh Eli." Mother looked at Buddy. "Don't be ludicrous."

"Going over at night, mostly. Sneaking out."

"Buddy? Is this true?"

Buddy had a way of paring his fingernails such that it was simultaneously a retreat and a meditation. Give him a knocking starter motor, a clunking U-joint, and out would come the pocketknife. A puff of breath on the blade, a slow, meditative curl of nail off onto his lap. He found the knife now, and started working on this thumbnail. "Seems so."

"Buddy? My daughter, my . . . my *fourteen*-year-old daughter?"

He studied his knife blade.

"You knew about this?"

"The last couple days is all."

"When were you going to tell me?" The skin had tightened across her cheeks. "No *wonder* Joyce Norton won't return my calls. Here I am trying . . . trying to . . . and here you are . . ."

Buddy showed her his palms, hauled out his best argument. "Mom was fifteen when she married Dad." For Buddy, the beginning and end of the discussion.

"You're comparing Emma to . . ." Mother stood stretched between impossibilities. A stronger person might have seen a solution. *Insisted* on a solution. State police, statutory rape, damn all you people.

My mother was not that person. She stood considering the best retort. The most suitable argument from the dozens that first came to mind. Considered each of them, then rejected each in its turn.

In the end, she did only what she could. That which she had always done when presented with impossibilities. She retreated. "I just can't . . ." Turned from us. Slid down the hall toward their bedroom. Shut the door softly behind her.

———

Emma spent the night at Pete's. If our mother hadn't already been starting one of her moods, this would have pushed her over the edge. Selfish, I thought. Then repeated it. Selfish, selfish, selfish.

The next morning, I was in the barn oiling leather harnesses, a set of old plow traces. From the driveway, the stutter of Pete's engine. He'd run any piece of machinery into the ground before springing for repairs. I was enjoying the mindlessness of my work. The smell of leather and oil. The soft jingle of buckles. Emma came up and stood above me, arms crossed over an open stall door. "Where is everybody?"

"Buddy's out checking on the heifers."

"Where's Mom?"

"Went to bed with a headache."

"One of *those* headaches?"

"I guess."

"Look at me, Eli."

"I'm working."

"You mad at me?"

"Whatever."

She stood there for a time. Chewed a nail, glanced around. Tilted her head at the plow traces puddled on my lap. Finally sighed theatrically. "I guess I might as well go back to Pete's."

"Fine."

"Might just stay awhile."

"Good."

"Well, all right then."

———

Pete hefted her luggage. "What all'd you bring here? The kitchen sink?" Emma was already thinking of this as her honeymoon. Silly idea, of course, but there it was. An occasion. And she'd always wanted to try marijuana. Somehow the two notions braided together in her mind: honeymoon, pot. Fixing his coffee, she said, "You wouldn't know where we could get some weed would you?"

"I got all kinds of wild mustard over on the old Hinkleman place."

"Oh, Pete. You're such a kidder."

It wasn't what she'd expected. How could it be? The nights were good. He still had some things to teach her. The way he scratched at her back: the light, circular caress of his nails. And the sex itself, which she had finally (finally!) come to enjoy. "We ain't worked our way through but about half of that Kama Sutra yet." But during the day, here's what he did: He blew his nose on the ground. Holding one nostril tight, he'd tilt his head to the side: Pthew. He had the habit of talking to himself, mumbling, cussing. Sonofoa*bitch*, he'd say for no good reason. He farted in bed and fluffed the sheets. He walked around the house in jockey shorts, crotch hanging loose. One time, working side by side, he cussed at her. They'd been pushing cows toward an open gate, trying to tell green ear tags from blue, and he yelled, "Jesus Christ, will you pay *attention?*" Asleep in bed, every part of him was vulnerable, exposed, soft as the underbelly of a toad. He would snort himself awake. A hawk, a spit. "Jesus, I got to ease off the booze."

There were good times, too, of course. When he pulled her struggling and giggling onto his lap, when she took a fencing tool from his hands to crowd herself into his arms. Times when neither was aware, nor particularly cared, that they were each on the receiving end of a capitulation.

Buddy's body filled the narrow hall. He stood turning his hat in his hands. "Maybe you can do something for her?"

Through the cracked door, mother lay with her eyes covered by a damp washcloth; arms stretched wide, hips twisted. The posture of crucifixion. The drapes were drawn, which was usual for one of her episodes, but she was mumbling, talking to herself, which was new. An endless loop of nonsense syllables. I drew back, shaking my head. "I've never seen her like this."

It was snowing again. A fluff, a few inches, finally a blanket, a shroud. Our familiar old woodpile slowly became a blunt white railcar. The house groaned under the weight of the snow. Buddy tilted a ladder to the eaves, sweeping fractured drifts to the ground. The storm felt like an angry act of nature. You are not wanted here, it said. We do not need you. "Maybe it's the electricity. Makin her crazy. What do you think." He shut off the main breaker with a metallic clunk, relegating our lives to the stone age. We played cards by candlelight, endless hands of rummy. "This country's always been hard on women. Don't know what it is. My old dad used to say it was the wind. Whose draw is it?"

"Yours."

He tilted his cards to the nearest candle, then studied the

discard pile. "No, see, you laid down a jack, and I already got me three jacks thrown down here for points, so you could take that and play it on mine. Ten points. I can't keep giving you all these free lessons." He took up a card from the deck. "Pete's mother. Woman could skin a deer, boil a pig, plant a garden. Grew these sweet old tomatoes. She liked to ride buckin horses and maybe that's how she put up with that sonofabitch she married, just rode him on down. Anyway, even she went crazy one time. Dad was driving home from Jordan and here comes Greta Fahler in a wedding dress, swinging a butcher knife. Said she was paying a visit to the place where your taxes go. Fifty miles, and she was going to go see about her taxes. Now, you just threw down a ten and that can go up top of this six seven eight nine over here. Pay attention."

Deeper in the house, in the darkness of her room, Mother lay curled under her quilts. Buddy had exiled himself to sleeping on the couch, but once or twice a day he would lie beside her, pulling her pale fist out from under the sheets, holding it to his chest, massaging the palm. She'd mumble an endless string of complaints, regrets. "I showed her oh she thought she was so special and then I said, like a bridge over troubled water I will lay me down, and why didn't you love me like you said you would when you said you would oh shit."

"I called Doctor Carl in Jordan, Bess. You remember Doctor Carl? Told him you were getting bad headaches and couldn't sleep. He said he could write a prescription if we needed it, but then I told him no, second thought, don't bother, you're already getting better."

She turned toward him. The oil of her unwashed face shone in the candlelight. She said, "What are you going to do about Emma?"

In discussing Mother, Buddy's vocabulary came straight from 1950s pop psychology. He'd found a textbook somewhere. "Is she subsuming, you think?" He had his pocketknife, trimmed at a thumbnail. Blew at it. "How about we get them over for supper, Pete and Emma. Get it all out in the open. What would you think about that?"

I hated the sound of it, *Pete and Emma*; the couplehood sound of it. But I felt oddly disconnected from what was in the midst of transpiring. I was not the grownup here. The decisions were not my responsibility. "Whatever you think."

That Saturday, Buddy washed dishes while I ran the vacuum. He stood at the stove, poking his spatula at a sputtering arrangement of frying pans, turning steaks while Tony lay on the kitchen table, popping teeth around a frozen bone. This was Buddy's bachelorhood, the loneliness that I'd never seen. When the car gate rattled, Buddy said, "That's them." He threw off Mother's apron. "You keep them busy. I'll call Abe on down."

The two of them stood in the mudroom, stepping out of their overshoes. Abe had come in through the back door. "Hey, Emma." Out of nervousness, Emma made much over him, giving him a hug. "Look at *you!*" At dinner, Abe sat happily in his habitual spot, napkin tucked into his collar. "Good to have you back, Emma." Buddy escorted Mother to the table like an invalid, bending close to catch a whispered question. "Why, no, Bess. It stopped snowing a couple days ago. Just look on out the window." She nodded, twisting at her wedding ring.

If Pete was startled by Mother's appearance (how *thin* she was, bedraggled; it had been days since she'd washed her hair), he didn't show it. "Whew-whee, I'm getting too old for these winters. Bess? Pretty as ever." Emma was wearing a tasseled buckskin vest. Around her neck an elk ivory pendant; on her smallest finger, a pearl ring, the stone ancient and shrunken and reset with glue. As we ate, she played with a curl of hair over Pete's ear. She grabbed his arm and giggled at the slightest of his jokes. She fed him pieces of steak from her fork. "Taste this, doesn't this taste good. What's that marinade you use Buddy?" Afterward, going to the stove for the coffeepot, Pete pinched her butt. She squealed and smacked him on the shoulder. "*Pete!*"

Outside, snowmelt dripped from the eaves. Buddy reached for his beanbag ashtray. "Reason we wanted you all to supper, Bess and me, we were just wondering what's next. What all you got planned."

Pete leaned back in his chair. "Hell, I don't make plans. You know that, Buddy."

"You two can't go on like this, Pete. You know how people talk." He pulled Mother's hand off her lap and folded it into his own. "Bess and me are worried."

"We're getting on just fine."

"What happens when we go to sell those calves and nobody wants nothing to do with you?"

"That ain't going to happen."

"It could."

Emma looked from Buddy to Pete. "Doesn't anybody want to know what I think?"

Pete drummed his fingers on the tabletop. "Might just go on forever. Hell, I don't know."

"You marrying her?"

Pete took a sip of coffee. "That's an idea, I guess."

Emma put her arm on the back of Pete's chair. "We've talked about it." She stroked his cheek with the back of her finger. "Maybe selling the ranch. Moving somewhere."

Buddy said to Pete, "Are you?"

"Am I what?"

"Marrying this girl."

"Can't say I won't."

"Are you?"

He paused. "Oh sure, hell, why not."

Emma squealed, and hid her face in his neck.

Was she misunderstood, was she wronged? I didn't give a shit. Chicken feeding and goat milking, her chores had become my chores. I told Buddy, "Pete can have her."

"Well, that's good. Since he's got her." Far as Buddy was concerned, the issue had been resolved. "Bess? You want a come on out, we can start planning the wedding. Bride's family pays, ain't that right?" After the wedding, any scandal would cease. We fed our cows and built fires in the stoves and the days passed. The community, according to its own complicated sense of etiquette and propriety, largely saved us the embarrassment of a confrontation.

Ms. Norton, however, wasn't part of the community. She sputtered into our yard on her little motorcycle, pulling off her gloves with her teeth. "Hey Eli. Mom and Dad home?"

Later, Buddy was polite but distracted. "Another cup of coffee, then?"

Ms. Norton said. "She's smart, Mr. Singer. She has a future. She's *fourteen*, for heaven's sake."

Buddy stirred a spoon into his coffee. "I guess they're going to be getting married."

"Married!"

"Talking about it."

"She's *four*teen, Buddy."

I was on the mudroom steps, sitting curled over my knees.

Buddy cleared his throat. "All due respect. I'm not sure this is any of your business, ma'am."

Ms. Norton's chair creaked as she leaned forward. "Burt Phillips called me for my opinion. *He* thinks it's my business."

"I won't have that now. Won't have the law involved, won't have the girl painted over with that brush. It's her decision. Theirs. Hers and his."

"Mister Singer." During her time in the Breaks, she'd accumulated a number of theories about Garfield County. About extreme isolation, and the effects it had on personalities; how it eroded certain sensibilities. Here was a girl with whom she'd identified. Bright, ambitious. And yet . . . this. It defeated her, saddened her.

"Yeah?"

She opened her mouth. Tried to choose a different tack, then visibly rejected it. Finally had to settle for denial. "I just don't understand."

I was constantly cold. Falling asleep, cocooned in quilts, this was the only time during the day when I was the least bit warm or comfortable. Whoever Buddy's mother might have been, whatever her failings, the woman had known how to make a quilt. Those thousands of tiny stitches. I dozed off listening to Buddy in the kitchen, playing his fiddle, scratching at a single note; a gentle, rocking-chair respiration of music. Later, after Buddy fell asleep on the couch, I would hear Mother's slump-slide of slippers, the small thump as her shoulder rested briefly against the wall. The yellow arc of a flashlight as it swung under my door, the rustle as she picked through the kitchen for a tube of crackers, a bag of chips.

In late January, I stood at the kitchen counter making lunch for school. Couple slices of bread, bologna, mustard. Left to my own devices, I would always have bologna sandwiches with mustard.

Mother came up behind me, pushing the hair out of her eyes. She wore jeans under her nightgown. Socks under her slippers. "I can get that for you."

I passed off the knife. "Are you feeling better?"

"A little."

"Well, that's good."

"I heard voices this time. A man's voice, all deep and raspy."

"What'd he have to say?"

She set the knife down. "You got a hug for an old lady?" She gathered me up in fleshless, clothes-hanger arms. "He told me, he said, Bessie, you got two kids. Now go and see about the other one."

The rest of her life, I don't remember another illness—no colds, no flus—nothing until her final complaint. "It's like I got a softball or something down in there." Maybe she eventually found a way to incorporate her headaches, embrace them. Maybe it's how you grow old, aging into a certain resignation.

In early February, Buddy paced back and forth in the kitchen, biting a pencil. "Okay, now, Eli, them heifers. Pete doesn't know just when they were bred so we need to keep an eye out. They're likely to start here any minute now. That's your job. Keep an eye on their vulvas. I'll help you." He made a shape with his two forefingers. "Plus, with all this heavy snow, I'm thinking we feed out cake. First thing tomorrow morning, we'll load up the flatbed, chain up all fours, go down into Wolfpen . . ."

There were footsteps on the porch, stomping snow. The door opened without a knock.

Emma stood there. Of course it was Emma. Thin legs in tight jeans, torso inflated by an unfamiliar blue down coat. She kicked the door shut and dropped her suitcase. Her expression was bored. Here we were, her beloved and despised family. Me with my hands half-swallowed in the sleeves of Buddy's old felt shirt. Mother still in a bathrobe, ink-dark circles under her eyes. She said, "Can I come home now?"

Mother said, "I saw this happening. Clear as day. I *saw* it. You were wearing that exact same coat."

Emma rolled her eyes. "I still got my room back there, right?"

Late February.

Mother and Emma were ignoring each other, so Mother had to piece the story together through phone gossip. "Is that right? I swear." Matty heard about Emma moving in, and started in with the pleading, the bargaining, the threats. "I'm not gonna stand by and see that little hussy marry into your ranch, Pete. She'll take it away from our kids, sure as the world. You get rid of her or I'm getting a lawyer."

Pete scorned the notion, but a seed of doubt had been planted. What were this girl's real motives? He was no spring chicken. What could she possibly see in him? She had all these questions. "How many acres you got here anyway?" It was only a matter of time until she caught pregnant. Oldest trick in the book. He'd always joked about selling out, going to Mexico, but that was just talk.

Finally, he kissed her on the cheek. "Maybe you should just go on back to Buddy's for a while. Give us some time."

And my sister. For all her swagger, her arrogance (real and feigned), she was still essentially a child. She had no real resources, no ready comebacks, no arguments. She was light enough to float at the mercy of the currents, the decisions made by others, by those whom she trusted. "Pete . . . ?" She cried a bit, and resisted his attempts at an embrace. She hit his shoulder. But what else could she do? Finally, she could only perform according to expectations. Could only follow the inevitable. She went back to Buddy's. She returned to us. If only briefly.

His heifers were polled Angus baldies, small and well-bred,

elegant in their shit-smeared way. But the bulls that had topped them, according to Buddy, must have been some kind of Charolais mutts. "I'd like to get my hands on that sorry-assed breeder. Saving a few bucks."

The calves, when they consented to come, were enormous, knob-headed mongrels, pale and spackled, the color of coffee with a drab of cream. Every uncrippled heifer seemed a miracle. How could a pelvis stretch so wide? One leg roped back and chains levered against her hips. The wash of fluid and the tips of hooves emerging like pale, cartilaginous knuckles. Buddy buried his hands up to his elbows, maneuvering. "That head hits the birth canal, sometimes the nose gets twisted back." Afterward, he would dig a finger into the calf's nostrils and, for good luck, blow a breath at the mouth. He brought the calf around to the mother. "Heifers get too skinny, sometimes they don't like their calves too much." As night calver, I was supposed to predict and subvert the disasters. Buddy said, "Something goes wrong, you can just come wake me up." It should have been fun, eight hours spent alone with a flashlight. But what if I woke him up and I was wrong? I hated being caught between choices, being the one responsible. We already had one dead cow in the yard, half-buried in a snow drift, legs cocked up like a tilted sawhorse. "They pinch that nerve sheath, it paralyzes the hips." She'd lain crippled for a few days, alert, occasionally struggling, but after her chin had dropped to the ground Buddy had gone for his rifle. He'd stood at a distance, aiming between her eyes, shifting his grip. "See if you can get her attention." Finally, he'd had to step around behind, holding the barrel inches from the knobby crest of her spine. He looked away to pull the trigger.

The walls of the calving shed were made of rough-hewn pine, warped and cracked. The gaps between boards made for fine finger holds. Late at night, I would sometimes climb the walls, inching up board by board until I could touch the ceiling. Heifers lay reduced in the stalls below me, chewing cud. I napped in the bunkhouse, a tiny cubicle partitioned away from the rest of the barn by a few sheets of loose plywood. I had a cot and a nightstand, a bureau with the drawers missing, a woven rag rug over the cement. Buddy had tossed me a sleeping bag: "Unroll your soogan there cowboy." An old tin alarm clock set at two hour intervals. Ten o'clock, twelve o'clock, two o'clock. I remember finding a heifer in the farthest corner of the pasture, her legs straddled and her head down, a dead calf dangling slick and pale between her legs, thin as a housecat. The barnyard mud melted and refroze. Shining my flashlight around at the dozens of sets of eyes, the paired reflectors, I wasn't even all that sure what I was looking for. "Somebody gets real close, you see them hooves pushing through, you come get me." But was that a hoof? Slipping in the mud, falling on my knees, it wasn't fair.

A week or so into my duties as night calver, I came back from a trip around the lot to find Emma waiting for me in the bunkhouse, cross-legged on my cot, reading one of Buddy's old *Playboys*. I'd found a sheaf of them under the cot. She spread out the centerfold. "You *like* this sort of thing?"

"What do you want?"

"Couldn't sleep." She twisted the magazine into a roll.

I had a speech waiting, a thousand times rehearsed. What's the *matter* with you. A roof over your head, somebody cooking your meals, a job. And you treat everybody like, like,

like we're strangers to you? Like we're nobodies? But confronted with her in the flesh, all I could manage was, "I don't want to talk to you."

"Why not?"

"I just don't."

She looked very young. I was prepared to forgive her. All it would have needed was some small gesture, a brief expression of regret, a single word. I missed you. I'm sorry. Instead, she said, "It was all Matty's fault." A cow shifted in the neighboring stall, splattering urine. "I've been giving him a little time. That's just what he said, right? Give me a little time. And now I have, and now he's just about ready to start regretting it. Don't you think? Right about now?"

I took the magazine from her, the tube of it, tossed it fluttering to the wall. I was being an adult, someone who didn't just forgive and forget, a man whose resolutions didn't falter, who made a judgment and stuck to it. "Not my business."

"You don't want to talk?"

"No."

"He said he loved me." She blinked hard, looking away. "Why would he say such a thing then tell me to just *leave*?"

"I got work to do."

"I've been thinking. We should go back to Billings. Just me and you."

"Emma."

"No, really. We could do it. It'd be easy."

"Easy?"

"Okay, you know that old hollowed-out Bible where Buddy keeps his emergency cash? Four or five hundred bucks there. So we take that, we take Mom's car, we go get us a motel room. It doesn't even have to be Billings. It could be Spokane. Or maybe even Seattle. We could just keep on going."

"What happens when the money runs out?"

"We get jobs."

"Who's going to hire a couple runaways?"

"We wouldn't be runaways. This isn't home. How could you run away from a place that isn't home?" She dropped back flat against the wall. "I just can't stay here anymore. I *can't*."

"Well, you have to."

"He said he loved me."

"I got to go check on the heifers."

"You just checked on them."

"I need to check on them again."

"You know what your problem is? Your problem, you don't ever want to take a chance."

"I'm not stealing, Emma. Stealing from Buddy? You're blaming me because I don't want to steal?"

"Well, *you* think of something."

"I like it here."

"Well me? I'm leaving." She was wistful. "I'm already gone."

What does a suicide want? William Gass asked the question and provided a response. Not what she gets, surely. In the years since Emma's death, I've persisted in the subjunctive. Would have, should have, could have. Thirty years I've spent trying to crack a spoon into the skin of my failure, create a seam in which to wedge the least sliver of rationalization. But no. She looked for me; I wasn't there. Her days unraveled, life wasn't what she'd hoped. She'd been misled. Here was the roof under which all other, lesser tragedies are contained. She drew pierced hearts across her notebooks and collected movie stubs in a drawer. Fourteen years old, she was not the person she aspired to be.

I'd been taking late night walks away from the calving shed. It was a small but significant rebellion. At first, ten minutes away just to stare at the stars. But then the ten minutes became an hour, then two hours. The ranch buildings were quiet behind me, dimly lit or not lit at all. Fifty miles to the nearest street light but here was Orion's belt, the big dipper, the Pleiades. Coming back to the barn, I would run my flashlight around the pasture, inspecting vulvas, singing low, "Oh black water, keep on rolling, Mississippi moon won't you keep on shining on me." Frozen mud crunched under my boots. It wasn't so bad, maybe; being a cowboy.

I let myself in the far end of the barn, listening to heifers shift in their stalls. "Anybody drop a calf while I been gone?"

I'd left my bunkhouse dark, but now there was a sliver of light under the door. "Buddy?" The door was held shut by its latch, a cheap metal hook of the kind that fastens restroom stalls. "Buddy? That you?" It had some give to it, and through the crack I could see a boot, the flesh of one thin leg. "Emma? Are you asleep in there?"

No response. I pushed in with my shoulder, widening the crack. An elbow, a braid of hair. A swatch of red pigment across her cheek.

"Emma?" I braced my feet and leaned hard against the door, pushing until the latch splintered loose, throwing me into the room.

She sat cross-legged on the floor, forehead against my mattress, left arm thrown off to one side, sliced open from elbow to wrist.

It had been so long since I'd seen real color, so many weeks of monochromatic winter, my first shock came from the vibrant, violating explosion of red. The wide puddle of it. My foot slipped, and I had to catch myself against the footboard. A kitchen paring knife, loose in her right hand. There was so much blood. It had soaked into the mattress. She couldn't still be alive. And yet, her chest rose slightly. "Emma?" Her right arm, still holding the knife, dropped to the floor. The blade clattered against the cement. It put me in motion. Okay, okay, first things first. Get her up on the bed. Sick people go into bed. Blood smacked under my boots. I swung her by the shoulders over onto the cot. The movement pushed a fresh hot trickle out of her arm. She mumbled now, her words urgent, barely audible: "Don't Eli, don't."

"It's going to be okay. It's going to be okay."

She turned her head toward me. Eyes dark and dull and enormous. She said my name. "Eli." A weak exhalation. Her head lolled back loose, exposing her neck, her fragile jaw. I put my arms under her legs, her back, and lifted her to the cot. It was like lifting an armful of cardboard, light but awkward. She made a low animal noise in the back of her throat.

I tied a tourniquet above her elbow, a tight twist of shoelace. Buddy would later compliment me on my clear-thinking. "Guess you did everything you could." When I lifted her arm, her skin was cold and the lips of the wound were bleeding only in the slow, gathering way of dew collecting on a pop can. Her eyes found me, and I held her head close to my chest.

My sister died just after three o'clock in the morning on February 24, 1979. Driving in the station wagon to Jordan, her head in my lap, my mother cradled Emma's arm. She mumbled, "I saw this I knew it I saw it coming I should have known I didn't want to believe it but I saw it. Just like this, just like this." Emma's arm had been wrapped in a torn section of a child's pink sheet. Something from Buddy's closet. It had a star pattern on it. An hour later, as they lifted her body free of the car, her neck had gone stiff inside my arm. I'd been sitting so long, I'd lost the feeling in my legs. I could only sit there as they took her from me.

The day of my sister's funeral, a cold breeze rattled at the cemetery's chain-link fence. Twenty or so mourners stood arranged on one side of the grave, facing away from the wind. The turnout was so small. Where were the rest of them? Emma had cleaned their houses, for Chrissakes. Was it guilt that kept them away? Were they reconsidering how they'd treated her? That had surely been part of Emma's motivation: *They'll be sorry when I'm gone.*

Her casket sat on an aluminum trolley above the open grave. It looked much too large for her small body. Below the cemetery, among the trailers at the edge of town, a dog barked, a man's voice rose against it. Beside the grave, a mound of fresh dirt had been hidden under a flapping green tarp. The preacher said, "Amen," and took half a step back. Six pallbearers, strangers to me, came forward to the leather straps, lifting the casket out over the hole. They lowered it hand over hand to the bottom, somber but hurried. The casket sat slightly askew in the bottom.

Buddy stepped forward to a spade hidden under the tarp, and shoveled the first measure of dirt into the grave. Gravel spattered across slick wood. He handed the spade to my mother who, trembling and uncertain, tipped a few cups worth of dirt into the hole. Her eyes raw as scabs. She was ten years older than she'd been the week before. If you're a parent, here it was. The worst thing. Her hat, a gray pillbox, sat aslant, held down with pins. She couldn't stop touching me, grabbing at my shoulder, my arm. Buddy put his big hand on my shoulder, pushing me forward. I took the shovel and dumped in the largest portion of dirt yet. That was Emma in there. My sister, eyes closed against a satin ceiling. She'd never move again. Never smile or laugh or cry. To a twelve-year-old boy it seemed a revelation, that the world had so little to offer us in the way of faith or promise or certainty. A box at the bottom of a hole.

Abe had come dressed in his father's shrunken black suit. The sleeves exposed an inch of white cuff, the pants rode up the side of his zippered boots. The shovel wasn't offered to him, but he stepped forward to take it from me, and tilted a measure of his own dirt into the grave. His hat was an old felt fedora, a size too large and packed inside with newspapers. Turning away from the grave, he stiffened. I followed his eyes. Pete Fahler sat idling in his truck outside the cemetery fence, alone.

Abe pressed his hat more firmly on his head and stalked toward him, weaving through headstones and plastic flowers. Pete started his truck. Abe stepped faster. Then ran. His hat went tumbling among the graves. Pieces of newsprint swirled and span around his feet. "You sonofabitch, you *sonofabitch*." Pete pulled away, tires spinning gravel. Abe stood panting, muscles clenched, a muddy glare for the world at large. Such a gentle man to contain such fury.

I resented it a little. That he'd had the capacity, the where-withal, to act.

That night, I woke to Buddy's fiddle.

I stepped out in my long johns. The lacquer of his instrument caught a sliver of blue light from the barnyard. Buddy sat staring at a crumpled piece of black fabric on the table, centered like a bouquet. I pinched it up in my fingers. A faint dust drifted down. Threads of ripped fabric, a pattern of faded stars. A hundred years ago, it had been wrapped around Emma's arm. A century before that, it had belonged to Buddy's sister, it had been the linen on her bed. He'd perhaps been dwelling on the confluence of these two tragedies. Little Emma. His sister.

I let the clump of fabric fall, wiping my hands on my drawers.

Buddy scratched soft and slow at his music. He swallowed hard, and tried to find something to say, some consolation in the mundane. "Old man Ballard said. He said. I guess we got us a dozen new calves. Haven't lost a one."

"That's good."

"I've been . . . sitting here. Thinking about Pete."

"Me too."

"What are you thinking?"

"It doesn't seem right, how he's just getting away with everything."

"It don't, does it." He scratched out a discordant flat on his fiddle. "Did you see this coming? Did you have any idea?"

"No."

"No. How could you." He laid the fiddle back in its case, clicking shut the lid. His manner was decisive. "You get to bed now."

"What are you going to do?"

"Nothing." He wadded up the strip of cloth and shoved it in his pocket. "Not a thing. But you go to bed."

Buddy gave it an hour. Long enough, presumably, for me to fall asleep.

But I knew Buddy well enough to recognize a decision when I saw one.

As he left the house, I followed close behind him. He started his truck. I waved my hands in front of his headlights. It was very cold.

He rolled down his window. "Get on to bed, Eli."

"You going over to Pete's?"

He hesitated. "I'm giving him a piece of my mind is all."

"I want to go with you."

"Probably not a good idea, Eli. What I got to say, this is between me and him."

"Emma's my . . . she was, was my sister. Please, Buddy?"

He scowled, considering. Little Eli, whom he was trying to raise to be a man. Finally, he said, "This is probably some kind of mistake. But okay, get on in."

We sat at idle, headlights splashed against his bedroom window. Maybe we were in a gangster movie. Maybe Buddy was my sidekick, or maybe I was his. He lit a cigarette. Cracked his window. The heater fan swirled at the smoke, pushed it toward the open window. After a time, a lamp glowed in Pete's house. We saw him part drapes and stand shading his eyes against the headlights. "About damn time." Buddy climbed out of the truck, glanced back. "You coming?"

When Pete's door opened, it threw a column of light across the yard. He squinted into the headlights. Called out, "Buddy? Something wrong with our heifers?"

"Heifers are fine."

"What's going on?" Pete stepped full into the glare of the headlights.

"You wronged us, Pete. You did wrong by Emma."

I came up beside Buddy. Pete looked at us both. "Hell, Buddy. Eli. I'm as sorry as can be about what happened. But I couldn't of known it, Buddy. Couldn't have known it."

This was the denial that Buddy had expected. "We don't believe you. Do we, Eli?"

"Nope."

Buddy extracted his right hand from his coat pocket. It snagged briefly, but when he freed it, it came out fisted around a pistol. The .44 from his shoebox in his closet.

Pete held up his hands. "Whoa, now. Just. Whoa, a second now."

In the harsh glare of the headlights, I had eyes only for Buddy. I admired him, I loved him. *Yes*, I thought. This.

Emotions rolled over the skin of his face. His brow twisted, his lips contorted.

Pete said, "I'm sorry, Buddy. There ain't no reason for this. Put that away now."

Buddy stood with the pistol held out, his arm stiff. It was an effort for him. He held his breath.

Was there ever a point when he intended to go through with it? In retrospect, no. I don't believe so. Not in the basement of his true intentions. If that had been the case, no way would he have allowed me to come along. No, I think he simply wanted to see Pete grovel, beg. Perhaps give me the gift of seeing Pete on his knees.

With an abrupt exhalation, Buddy let his arm fall. "I can't, Eli." He turned, and laid the pistol on the hood. He hunched his shoulders, braced. "I can't."

Pete said, "Jesus, Buddy. You had me going there for a second." His relief gave way to self-righteousness. "You came here to shoot me? What the hell are you thinking?" And self-righteousness segued, in the next breath, to default arrogance, to gloating. "Can't believe you'd think you had the balls for such a thing. I knew you didn't have the balls. Knew it all along."

I maneuvered around Buddy. Stood on tiptoes to reach up over the hood.

His pistol was heavier than I would have imagined. But it had a balance to it. It tried to adjust itself to my hand. A big gun, it was slightly too large for me. Brass cartridges winked around the outside edge of the cylinder.

I was already considering the circumstances of a cosmic censure or approval. I was looking for a sign. If Pete begged me for forgiveness, if he got down on his knees, I'd put the gun away. If Buddy touched my shoulder, if he pulled me back, I'd put the gun away. If the headlights flickered at just the right moment, if god gave me a message, I'd put the gun away.

I wrapped both hands around the grip, still warm from Buddy's pocket, and pointed the pistol at Pete.

"Now it's your turn? Give it a break, boy."

I couldn't talk to him; I couldn't say his name. He was not Pete Fahler. He was not. I focused on a spot below his chin, above his breastbone. Graying chest hairs tufted out above his T-shirt. My arms trembled. Maybe I was still making up my mind.

My forefinger curled against the trigger.

I squeezed hard, flinching against the coming kick.

It didn't come.

I squeezed harder. Still nothing. The muscles in my forearm would hurt the next day, that's how hard I squeezed. Not even a click. The effort must have shown in my face, however, because Pete jerked away, flattening his hands across his chest. Then he recovered, "Ha. That's a pretty good one, Eli."

Behind me, Buddy said quietly, "It's a single action. You got to cock it first."

Was this what he wanted? Was it what he expected? My cheeks were numb in the cold, hard as plastic. There were all those stories Buddy liked to tell. Men with fists the size of hams, gun battles and misfired rounds. He whupped him; he whupped his brother; his brother whupped him back. Odd for such an otherwise gentle soul. "Old Lou thrashed him until he didn't have no teeth at all." This would be something he and I would share. Nothing, not our work on the ranch, our shared despair at Emma's suicide, not his marriage to my mother, nothing would bind us so tightly as this.

Was it revenge? I could anticipate none of the satisfaction you might expect from revenge. I remember instead a sense that a distasteful job would shortly be falling behind me. There were certain expectations on the table.

Pete said, "Eli? I'm saying I'm sorry? Doesn't that mean anything? C'mon now, son." In the bitter cold, his bare arms had turned a chapped, glowing red.

The pistol was harder to cock than I would have thought. Maybe the grease in the mechanism had stiffened up in the cold. I wedged the barrel between my knees and levered the hammer back. Click-click.

Pete might have stepped forward at this point, grabbed the pistol from me, but he was still being reasonable, still convinced of his own virtue. "Hell, Eli. She come to me. I didn't have nothing to do with it. First time? She let herself into my house, crawled right into my bed. What was I going to do? What's a man to do?" He grinned again. "You ain't serious about this."

And so then I shot him.

I don't remember aiming. Don't remember raising the pistol. I pointed it at him and curled my finger. And just that easily, I became Pete's punctuation. His whole life, I was the exclamation point at the end of his story. It was always going to be me.

———

What were his crimes after all? Nothing more (I'm sure he believed) than the failures of the human condition. Animal attraction. In his final moments, he must have felt the greatest sense of injustice.

I closed my eyes. When I opened them, he had fallen back onto the ground, splay-legged, tilted back on one arm. His mouth worked at a silent vowel, slack and bloody. The other hand had gone to his chest. Blood trickled black between his fingers. As Buddy and I watched, his elbow went unhinged, easing him flat back into the snow. He stared at me, and then at the gun in my hands. Such a big pistol for such a small boy.

Buddy said, "Shoot him again. Make it quick, for Christ's sake."

His warm blood eroded at the drifts of snow around him. They collapsed, eaten at from underneath.

"Shoot him again, I said. Make it quick."

Pete coughed, and cupped a hand to his mouth, catching bloody foam. A faint, two-toned whistle rose from the hole in his chest.

"Chrissake." Buddy snatched the pistol from me and stalked forward, a man set to an unpleasant task. He placed the barrel inches away from Pete's temple. Pete stared up, dull with shock, coughing weakly.

The barrel shook.

Pete's gaze went to Buddy, then back to me.

It was all leaking away, Pete's life. His wife and her wincing pain the first time they'd made love. His little girl, who had held the entirety of his sorrow. His son and his toy trucks, his son for whom he'd entertained such extravagant hopes. All of it was going. And yes, my sister; and yes, me and Buddy, his ranch. All of it.

His own damned fault, I thought. But did not entirely convince myself.

Buddy turned away, the pistol at his side. The next shot was beyond him.

I had exceeded him, or failed him.

Eli, his stepson, the murderer. I was a murderer now. And would be from this moment forward.

Pete stiffened, heels digging at the snow. He squinted past me, unfocused. He shivered against the cold and loss of blood. The shivers turned to spasms. Hard tics. His head lolled to one side and his teeth clattered. A tendril of blood trickled from his mouth. He looked at his own curled fingers in the snow. He fixed on his fingertips, watched them flex, and stretch, then curl loose.

Then he quit breathing. Quit blinking. Quit trembling. He quit.

After burying Pete down in Cherry Creek, we came back for his keys. I waited on the porch. Buddy emerged carrying the ring of keys and a wad of paper towels. "Fingerprints," he said, scrubbing the towels around the knob. I admired his clear thinking. We were going to be okay. Buddy and me, we were going to get through this. He said, "You think you can drive my truck back to the house?"

"Sure."

"I'll follow behind in Pete's truck. We'll need to get rid of it. Make people think he's left town. Ashamed about Emma, and whatnot."

"Where would we hide it?"

"Canyon Reservoir, I'm thinking."

I followed along behind, driving carefully, sitting stretched half off the seat in order to reach the gas pedal. Ten minutes later, Buddy drove through our yard on his way to the reservoir. I'd thought he might want to wait until dawn. But no. He had a job to do? He wanted to get it done.

We stood together above the Canyon Reservoir, Pete's truck idling beside us. Clay cliffs angled down at our feet. Seventy, eighty feet of runneled soil scraped raw. Buddy broke off a dead branch and wedged it tight over the gas pedal. The engine revved. He straightened the wheel and eyed the trajectory, made a small correction to the steering wheel. "Step out of the way now." He dropped it into gear. The truck's tires spun briefly in the snow, then caught. The vehicle leapt forward, the open door banging against Buddy's back. It gathered speed, finally to tilt over the edge. A pause, then a shattering of ice, a crumpling of metal. We stepped forward to watch. It had hit on its roof. Cracks radiated away. It sank slowly, finally to disappear.

I said, "So we got away with it?" I looked at him. I wanted a smile, a pat, a brief hug of reassurance.

Buddy's thick face was expressionless. He hunched further inside his big coat. "Nobody gets away with nothing."

Buddy saw it coming. "We'll have a few days, get our stories straight, then all hell's going to break loose." Living alone, an aged bachelor, Pete had been largely beyond community acceptance or concern. "Boys will be boys and men will be worse." He was known to frequent certain bars in Miles City, for instance. More than once, Matty had driven down to Billings with bail money folded in her purse. But he'd never left in the winter before, never ignored his ranch. He skipped his weekend visit with Curt, and anyway, where was Matty's alimony check? One day, then two, and he still wasn't answering his phone. *Bastard*. Matty drove out from Jordan to find the mail clumped in his box, a drift of snow crusted across his porch. The tracks of our truck, of our own feet, were almost gone, the pieces of them scattered here and there, old as archaeology. After a thaw and another couple inches of snow, his blood was a distant, frozen smear. Unnoticed. A spill of antifreeze, maybe. Inside, she heard the sound of dripping water from a burst pipe. Walking to the phone, she left soggy tracks in the carpet. Waiting for the sheriff, she turned off his water main, picked up his dirty clothes. Finally, she sat on a corner of his bed and sipped instant coffee, smoothing the quilts back and forth. *Bastard*. She began to cry.

Maybe he'd had an accident out on the ranch. Burt and his deputy, Frank Nye, drove the roads and ridges, craning their heads into the ravines. Lukewarm coffee from a thermos, and the sheriff's mild complaints about Nye's smoking. "Them things are gonna kill us both." He rolled down his window. They were looking for the undercarriage of Pete's truck, maybe a set of taillights in the trees. "You remember old Loren Finney, how he got kicked in the head that time?" The most likely scenario, Pete with a shotgun in his mouth, went unspoken. Maybe he'd walked off drunk and froze to death. That sort of thing happened time to time. Volunteers arrived from town. Pete's yard became a parking lot. Trucks idled fender to fender, puffing exhaust. Tires pressed his hidden blood further down into the driveway dirt, into dead grass.

Some of the volunteers wore hunter's orange, some carried walkie-talkies. Buddy and I walked among them, eventually to stand by ourselves on a sandstone outcropping above Cherry Creek. We could see over the fence into our own ranch. Could, in fact, see the exact spot where Pete was buried.

"Buddy?"

"Yeah."

"I'm, uh." I found it difficult to say. It took me a few tries. Then: "Sorry. I've been thinking that I guess I need to say that. I'm sorry."

Buddy hunkered over his heels. Between his feet, a patch of sandstone blown bare of snow. He took up a handful of rock pieces and began to grind them between his big fingertips, turning them each to dust. "Yeah." He sifted the dust palm to palm. "Me too."

"Feels like we're lying, kind of. Doing all this. Looking for Pete and all."

"Yes it does." He dusted off his hands.

I had thought the violence against Pete would unite us, would bring us together. "Buddy . . . ?"

"Yeah?"

"Nothing."

He stood up. "We'd better get on. Can't make it look like we're lazy."

The disappearance remained an irritation. For thirty years, it was an unanswered question, a narrative punctuated only with an ellipse. The final evening of the search, there was beer around a campfire, steaks grilled on Pete's barbeque. Laughter. "Hell, he's probably kicking it on some California beach about now." Within the week, Matty was back serving whiskey Cokes at Hell Creek Bar. Tips were better than they used to be.

After we sold the heifers that fall, we sent her a check for Pete's half. She never acknowledged it.

Trapped in the soil, Pete began his slow dissolution.

The evening after the search was called off, Buddy sat alone with a bottle of Jim Beam. He'd found it rolling around on Pete's floorboards but hadn't touched it until now. He'd worked it down to near empty. He tilted it to the light. "Say what you want about Pete Fahler, he knew his booze." He turned it in his hands. "So what's it feel like, to kill a guy?"

It made me uncomfortable. That Buddy should ask me a question. More than uncomfortable. It represented a paradigm shift in who he was, who I was. That I might have some awareness, some experience, that was beyond him. I wasn't ready for it, not yet. "It doesn't feel like anything."

"No?"

I clarified. "It feels like nothing."

"Well, I'm sorry for you."

"Sorry for what."

"You got seventy, eighty years ahead of you. A whole lifetime of living with it. Worst thing a man can do. It's going to be tough."

It hadn't occurred to me that he might feel pity. Anything but pity.

A few years ago I sat in a bar in Miles City, listening to an old man on a packing crate stage scratch at an undersized fiddle. He had a soft, swollen nose and five-dollar dentures, and cradled the fiddle against one bicep, grinning his way through *Fox on the Run* and *Angel Band*. I dropped five single-dollar bills into a straw cowboy hat and knuckled at my eyes.

There's a photo on my bureau. Mother and sister, arm in arm. If you let your eyes uncouple, you will see one woman, doubled. Cocked hips and bent elbows. My mother was eighteen when she had Emma, and couldn't have been more than thirty-one when this photo was taken. But she looks older, her face drawn, ruined. My sister smiles with the jaded genius of adolescence. She thinks she owns the world and maybe she does. A denim jacket with a damp chewed collar and clumsy makeup around the eyes. You can tell, you can see it already. Here's a girl who will crack hearts with a smile.

It wasn't that she left, it was only that she left me behind.

I was born on the sixteenth of March, Emma on the eighteenth. Every year on the seventeenth, it had been Mother's habit to bake us a shared cake and pour herself a glass of wine, and say, "Two Pisces in the same house, no wonder, no wonder." After Emma, after Pete, what would be left of the ritual? The evening of the sixteenth, Mother brought out a chocolate cake. "Surprise, there, birthday boy." A lopsided attempt, the icing full of crumbs.

I had a present, a hunting knife. It would have been Mother's idea. She lit a single, over-large dinner candle, and forced a smile. "Better hurry before it melts into the icing." Buddy sat back, silent. What was he thinking? What was going through his mind. I could not read him.

Mother began singing "Happy Birthday." Buddy shifted his gaze to her until she finally trailed away. I sat for a time, waiting for someone to tell me again to blow out the candle.

Buddy pushed back from the table. Found his hat. "Well I guess that's it then."

Horace says that anger is a brief insanity. *Ira furor brevis est.*

Having gotten away with the worst, some men would, I think, be tempted to continue down the same path. Explore the possibilities of violence. For others, it might send them off into a lifetime of penance. Me, as far as I can tell, I've found my consolation in the Breaks, the ten thousand shades of blue in the sky, tree bark the color of dried blood, the squabbling of birds, and the rotation of stars; poetry.

Buddy shrank into his old age. He lost weight and his hair.

Mother grew rounder, firm as an apple. Buddy's intermittent withdrawals, his inexplicable resentments, did not seem to damage his marriage. In photos, they're always touching. A hand on a shoulder, Mother's finger hooked through his belt loop. They had each other.

But I did not have them. This isn't self-pity so much as observation. Guilt isolates. I believe there's biology to it. Downcast eyes, reticence, scowls, muttering. It's a virus, an infection. The herd tends to avoid melancholy. Where's the evolutionary advantage in spending your days with some self-absorbed asshole?

When I can't sleep, as a meditation, an exercise, I'll imagine that she's still alive. She ran away, she made it to Portland, Seattle. The wind knocks against the door, and maybe it's Emma, stamping her boots. Or maybe she's watching TV in a Vancouver apartment, one child playing blocks on the floor, another at her breast, considering the phone, wondering if she should call. Maybe she's working toward a graduate degree, or scribbling orders on a pad, "How you want that cooked?" Growing older, she would accept invitations to drink from a series of increasingly jaded men. Now and then she'd spare a thought for her abandoned brother in Garfield County. She would never change in his eyes. Would that be satisfying to her? That there was still a small corner of Montana where Emma the teenager was even now lying on her bed, playing Billy Joel eight-tracks, kicking bare heels together.

Who we are is where we are. The stars cross and align and the days pass.

Buddy died eight years ago. We were moving cows and I

lost him in the dust. As it cleared, I saw his horse standing a quarter-mile behind, head down, reins trailing. I found him with one hand clawed on his chest, the corners of his mouth stretched wide. An expression of painful ecstasy. It recalled certain jazz trumpeters, gospel singers.

Five years earlier, he'd bought Mother a satellite dish. One of those ponderous alien saucers that landed overnight next to a million trailer houses. Mother loved it. "I just appreciate the company." She called Bob Barker by first name and fell in love with Donahue and dialed 800 numbers for steak knives and colanders and blenders. In the years before her own death, she took to quoting the title of her favorite soap opera. Staring into Buddy's open grave, she said, "The world keeps on turning, don't it Eli?" When she herself lay in a Billings hospital, stomach bile draining green through a tube in her nose, a cross-hatched stitching of scars across her abdomen, she whispered, "The world's still turning though, eh Eli?"

Indeed, the world turns, hauling us with and within it, living and dead alike. Regrets come to us like nails to a magnet: an unfortunate word that ends a friendship, an ill-timed insult that cripples a marriage. And still the world turns. We search for lovers and friends, companions who might see past our insults, partners to whom we'll be able to finally confide. But she doesn't come, they haven't come, and so we settle; until those for whom we've settled are precisely those for whom we've been waiting. We reproduce the days, the years, hoping always for a fresh start, for a new face in the mirror, for last year's bad choices to spring new again. But they haven't come, and still they haven't. And so we're finally left to wonder if it's been enough, if we've done everything that was expected of us. We don't know, we can't, and yet still the world turns. And our first consolation, our only real comfort, is that it has never before turned this far around.

The Coyote, Part II

Careful of the blood, I draped him
across a sheet of plywood, unzipped
him belly to chin, sliced the pelt away
until his lipless skull grinned up, sharing
the oldest joke in the world.

Either everything is forgivable, I thought,
or nothing is.

Who we are is where we are. She considers the line.

Singer in New York. Which means . . . what, exactly?

He keeps his cowboy boots—broken at the arch, splitting at the toe—under the dracaena. A plant she had bought him as a housewarming present. They aren't living together but might as well be. He'd found a studio apartment on the edge of Gowanus and Park Slope. A view of the BQE from one window, a fringe of distant cemetery trees from another. Bare brick walls. The guy's in New York ten minutes, he finds the perfect apartment. "You're making me jealous, Singer." A baseball cap that advertises seed and Wranglers with snoose rings worn into the hip pockets. A coiled riata hanging over deer antlers. None of it calculated, none of it artificial. The last authentic man in New York.

They're a couple, sure; they're committed to each other, exclusive (after blood tests, no more condoms), but she still finds his privacy irritating, his kneejerk urge toward self-containment a sliver of popcorn in her teeth. She can't leave it alone. "One of these days you're going to have to learn to open up, Eli."

"I open up."

"Maybe you could be the one to *start* a conversation, for instance."

"Why would I want to go and do *that*." A lopsided grin, but truth in the humor.

Evenings, they walk Dante and Beckett (muzzled) the three-mile circuit around Prospect Park. She keeps glimpsing Glen Sweete. That dark blue suit, the white cowboy hat. In a crowd on a subway platform, waiting in line at the Co-op. That guy's too short, the next one a little too heavy. It has become a very private burden. What happens when they interview Abe? Would the old man have the wherewithal to keep his insults contained?

Coming back into his apartment, the dogs make their habitual circuit around the inside walls, corner to corner, verifying once again that this is all the room they're going to have. Ranch dogs sentenced to a city. "What are you working on these days?" Singer's yellow legal pad on the table.

"Oh hell. Not much. Writing a letter."

"A letter?"

"To Abe."

"Mind if I read it?"

He considers her. "Why not."

Uncomfortably, aware of the impropriety of it (but unable to help herself), she brings the pad her way. Singer has begun without a salutation. "Not sure if you got my last note ..." Then he offers a brief description of the neighborhood, their days together ("The dogs can't figure out why I keep having to pick up their leavings in plastic bags"), and finally a plea for forgiveness. "Hoping one of these days you'll have it in your heart ..." She pushes the pad back toward him. "He hasn't replied?"

"Not yet."

"I'm sorry."

"Is what it is."

Later that same day, the afternoon air cold for April, they're on a bench in Prospect Park, sipping coffee, watching joggers. And he says, "I finally talked to that lawyer you been badgering me about." Singer, unshaven in a wool scarf and watch cap. For the first time since she's known him, he *looks* the part. Like he's a poet.

"Somebody here in New York?"

"Billings." The sun finds a crack in the clouds, and he squints up against it. In a certain light, at a certain angle, you can see the wrinkles that map his face, the shallow craquelure. A brief glimpse of the face he'll have when he's eighty. "Turns out, this guy's opinion, I can't be liable for Buddy's actions. Ain't a jury in the world would give Curt consideration. His opinion."

"So, that's good news, yeah?"

"Anybody can sue anybody for anything, but yeah, sure." He takes her hand. "I suppose."

Singer's manuscript is still on her nightstand. The title page stained over with coffee rings, red wine drips, a circular doodle of the sort she's inclined to draw while on the phone. The first third is punctuated with the marginalia of her profession. Encouragement, questions. "Beautiful imagery!" And, "Should this be presented earlier?" The last third, however, has been left blank. She read with the pen forgotten in her hand.

The month before, the day he had closed on his apartment, they'd had a celebratory dinner on Smith Street. Later, sitting on the platform at Atlantic, he'd said, "You finished my book yet?" He'd been rehearsing the question.

"If I still have the energy, I'll finish it tonight. Okay?"

"You'll want some time later."

He made it a point to hurry to bed ahead of her. She sat in her recliner, turning pages, drinking a final glass of wine.

An hour later, she sat staring into the mirror of her darkened window.

She'd thought that New York had hardened her. But no. Turns out (so naive), she was still just one big exposed nerve. Flinchy.

Honesty, by god. Jesus. And she'd asked for it, argued for it. And having asked for it, how could she now reject it? She couldn't. I mean, how?

But what was she now? What did this make her? Perhaps she forgave him. She touched the manuscript. Love, yes, but guilt, too. Perhaps they were complementary opposites. Not hate on the other side of that coin but rather guilt. You and me against the world, Singer. The manuscript would have to go in a safe deposit box, of course. Something to be opened upon their deaths. She could see how it might eventually become an elastic band pressing them together. The subtext of every argument, every tantrum, the manuscript in their shared box.

And Buddy. Eli a failure in his father's eyes. Eternally, a disappointment. What would it do to a guy, going through life with that idea?

Coming into bed that night, she found him still awake. He said, "Well?"

"I've just been thinking."

"About what?"

"About the affinity between poetry and lying." She sat in a chair across from the bed, hands on her lap.

"I'm not lying. Not now, anyway."

"How would I know? How do I know for sure?"

He came out of bed in his underwear, sat cross-legged on the carpet at her feet. "You don't, of course." He took her hand, her loose knuckles. Kissed her fingertips. "Maybe you have to trust me."

And yes, there it was. The gist of it. *Trust.* This, and not much more. It needed a tattoo. "What do you want from me, Singer?"

"I don't know. I truly don't."

"Well."

"Maybe you could tell me it's all going to be okay? Might be nice just to hear it, even if it's not true."

The next morning, he arose before her—he would always be the first out of bed—and left her a poem. A folded piece of paper beside a mug of coffee going cold.

> Before you found me
> I flapped loose as
> laundry on a line, empty
> shirt, wrinkled trousers
> waiting for limbs. You are
> my limbs, the hands
> that brought me down.
> I am in your hands.

In bed that night, he said, "I imagine it's like pneumonia patients, cancer patients. When they take a hypodermic and suck fluid out of your lungs. How you'd all of a sudden be able to breathe again." He placed her palm flat on his chest, showing her the motion of his lungs. "How it feels to pass something like this along."

Was that what he'd done? Passed it along? The burden of it. Guilt doesn't disappear, you just hand it on down the line.

She can see now how it might go with her. The thick interior poling through canals of evasion, rationalization. With this between them, they will become one of those irrevocable couples. The damnedest thing. There is oblique talk of marriage. He says at some point, "Wives can't be forced to testify against husbands."

If you needed one word to describe their couplehood, it would be *gradual*. They're settling into each other with the creaks and pops of a fresh foundation, leather shoes coming to terms with new corns. He still has his preoccupations, holdovers from his time alone (nobody else in Brooklyn, for instance, cares so much about moisture; he keeps a crude rain gauge attached to the flashing outside his window), but he has gradually stopped snagging on her cleavage. He has ceased to worry about the next terrorist attack. He laughs out loud. Weekends, she plays tour guide until he grows tired of the pandering. "How many times have I met you at that station on Forty-Ninth? You need to stop telling me where that's at." Her soft hand creeps periodically into his. They explore together . . . the crevices of their own bodies, the banks of the Hudson.

"Are you happy?" she asks.

Maybe. If that's what this is, yeah. But it's a new experience. The loss of himself into her ambitions, inhibitions, prejudices, joys. He has given up his old spiral notebook for something with a board cover and built-in rubber band. It's slightly too large for his shirt pocket, so he carries it in his fleece vest, along with an expensive Parker fountain pen she'd bought him for his birthday. During the day, while she's at work, he has taken to exploring the subway lines. This morning he took the N train to Coney Island. Walked the boardwalks, cowboy boots clocking against the wood, listened to the waves. He's not been writing much poetry but figures maybe it's time. The competing metronomes. His boots against the push and pull of waves. The gray scrim of waves. A tired conceit, sure, but new to him.

That night, he has Chinese takeout waiting for her. A nice red, breathing. "I saw this old woman on the train today. She was wearing flip-flops, and she had these toenails sticking out. Must have been about two inches long. Just think about that. How hard it would be to go through your day trying to tolerate two-inch toenails."

"You'd have to work at it, that's for sure." She's been growing her bangs, and can't stop trying to hook the stray hair over an ear. It's become a tic. He resists the urge to do it for her. To reach across and tuck away her hair.

It's a common thing, of course, this kind of story. Their lives bleeding into each other. But Singer is about ready for a common story. The twelve-year-old boy considers marriage. And then? A natural progression, maybe they'll walk slow around Prospect Park, Chloe swaying with the final months of her pregnancy, steadying herself on his arm.

He uses his one hand to rearrange the chopsticks in the other. Pokes around at a sodden piece of broccoli. Bringing it to his mouth, he glances across and finds her studying him. She smiles slightly, and brings her own piece of broccoli to her mouth. Outside on the street, a honking of horns, a distant siren. Some five-minute city tragedy passing quickly, nothing to them. Within the warmth of his apartment, he shares the moment, and feels it being shared. This moment, and then the next, then the potential for more. It's all so fleeting, of course, but those are the terms. Fleeting, or nothing.

They have a sense, both of them, for the many ways this could all go right.